THE BIG WANDER

Books by WILL HOBBS

Changes in Latitudes

Bearstone

Downriver

The Big Wander

Beardance

Beardream

Kokopelli's Flute

WILL HOBBS
THE BIG WANDER

ALADDIN PAPERBACKS
New York London Toronto Sydney

First Aladdin Paperbacks edition November 2004

Copyright © 1992 by Will Hobbs

ALADDIN PAPERBACKS
An imprint of Simon & Schuster
Children's Publishing Division
1230 Avenue of the Americas
New York, NY 10020

Also available in an Atheneum Books for Young Readers hardcover edition.

Printed in the United States of America
2 4 6 8 10 9 7 5 3 1

The Library of Congress has cataloged the hardcover edition as follows:
Hobbs, Will.
The Big Wander / Will Hobbs.—1st ed.
p. cm.
Summary: Although his older brother decides to return home to Seattle,
fourteen-year-old Clay continues his search for his uncle through the ruggedly beautiful
Southwest canyon country.
ISBN 0-689-31767-0 (hc.)
[1. Southwest, New—Fiction. 2. Uncles—Fiction. 3. Horses—Fiction. 4. Navaho Indians—
Fiction. 5. Indians of North America—Fiction.] I. Title
PZ7.H6524Bi 1992
[Fic]—dc20 92-825
ISBN 0-689-87070-1 (Aladdin pbk.)

For my mother

For my father

I'm glad I shall never be young without wild country to be young in. Of what avail are forty freedoms without a blank spot on the map?

—ALDO LEOPOLD

Map by: Virginia Norey

1

Clay Lancaster rolled the window down and drank in the wind and the rolling red desert, the clouds impossibly tall in Arizona's turquoise sky. He read the billboards aloud to his brother Mike at the wheel of the pickup.

PRAIRIE DOG VILLAGE!

GENUINE INDIAN MOCCASINS!

LIVE TWO-HEADED CALF!

Clay had never seen so many billboards in his life as lined Route 66. Dozens, even hundreds, advertised the same few roadside attractions. You started seeing the signs hundreds of miles away and you came to think of them as companions on this thin strip through the big emptiness.

Ahead, a long-promised trading post appeared on the red horizon, with a dozen tepees circling a cluster of gift shops disguised as a fort.

"Chief Yellowhorse Village coming up, Mike. Hey, that last sign said something about rattlers. Slow down."

"Slow down—that's a good one," his brother Mike said

with a smile, coming a bit out of the daze he'd been in ever since they left Seattle. "Clay, we could've raced a tortoise into Arizona and lost."

"C'mon, Mike, your Studebaker has character." To Clay everything about their trip was perfect, even the way the truck backfired going down the hills. They were on the loose at last and four days into the Big Wander.

"These places are all phony as wooden nickels," Mike scoffed. "The Indians in the desert didn't live in tepees."

"There it is again—BABY RATTLERS—hey, Mike, let's take a look at 'em! I bet it's time to check the oil again anyway."

It was always time to check the oil. They'd left a plume of blue smoke behind them all the way down through Washington State and Oregon and practically the whole length of California. The truck was new, bought especially for this summer out of Mike's savings for seventy-five dollars. Well, not exactly new, Clay thought, but new for them. Its original red showed in places, but mostly you'd have to say it looked rusty, which came close to matching the color of the desert and seemed a lucky thing at the moment. Another lucky thing about the truck was its age, Clay thought, it being a '48 model, same as me, and that makes us both fourteen.

They walked onto the wooden porch of the trading post and Clay's eyes looked past the cigar store Indian to the footlocker with BABY RATTLERS spelled out large. As Clay knelt and cautiously began to lift the lid, a pair of little boys came streaming out of a station wagon and bounded onto the porch, their parents trying in vain to call them back. Twins, Clay figured. They froze big-eyed as Clay peered through the opening into the box. "These rattlers are a little different from the ones back home," he reported to Mike. "Maybe they're desert rattlers."

A little smile came to Clay's face as he looked from his

brother to the buzz-headed twins, crowding as close as they dared, deliciously terrified and hair-triggered to run. Their older sister was stepping onto the porch, curious to find out what was going on.

"Careful," Mike warned.

Clay's right hand started into the box. The blond girl and her little brothers gasped.

"Clay!" Mike shouted.

"I think I can get one behind the head," Clay said calmly, and his arm disappeared inside the box. The twins took two steps back and eyed their escape routes. Even Mike backed up a little.

Clay reached inside, carefully, carefully. Suddenly it wasn't so easy for anyone to tell what had happened, with all the rattling and commotion and Clay's elbow flying back. But the sudden look of terror on his face said it all—he'd been bitten!

Now, Clay thought, crying out in pain and throwing the lid open, springing in one motion on the twins with two of the rattlers in his right hand. The boys screamed and fell back against their sister and their parents who were backpedaling nearly as fast, until they all spied the baby rattles in Clay's hand—a pink one and a blue one.

"Hey," one of the twins exclaimed, "those are *rattles*, not *rattlers*!"

By now everyone was laughing with relief. The twins took the rattles from Clay's hand, wanting to hold the "snakes" too and shake them menacingly. Clay was much more aware of their sister, who looked to be about his age. She was watching him, and she was smiling. Her glistening hair, curling into a flip at her shoulders, shone about as bright as the sun.

"Are you fellas on your own?" their father inquired. Clay had never met a Texan before, but he recognized the accent from the movies.

"We sure are," he answered proudly. "My name's Clay and this is my big brother Mike and we're on the loose."

Both parents looked a little confused. "You're on the loose," the mother repeated, sounding a little concerned.

Mike was standing back and seemed to be enjoying this. Clay thought he'd better explain. "We've been talking about a big trip for a long time, just the two of us, for the summer after Mike graduated. He's starting college in the fall—at the California Institute of Technology."

The man whistled and raised his eyebrows. "Good school."

"Where're y'all from?" the girl he liked asked cheerfully. Her hair was blonder than blond. To his amazement, she was speaking to him.

"Seattle," Clay answered, enchanted with her accent and hair and everything about her. She was shining that warm, sweet smile on him.

She must be wearing perfume, he thought, and as they started to talk he could feel its delicate scent wafting through his nostrils and overcoming his brain, making him dizzy. Tropical flowers, that's what it is. Like they have in Hawaii.

A miracle was happening. He was usually so shy with girls. . . .

Her name was Marilyn, which awed him, because the only Marilyn he'd ever heard of was a blonde too, and her name was Marilyn Monroe. As they talked, he started remembering Marilyn Monroe in one of the most memorable scenes of one of his favorite movies, *River of No Return*. He could see her now, struggling to keep her feet on that lurching makeshift raft out in the middle of the rapids. He'd often pictured himself rescuing a girl in just such a situation and earning her eternal gratitude.

4

2

By a great stroke of luck, her father wanted to treat him and Mike to milk shakes at the soda fountain, and in a heartbeat Clay was sitting next to Marilyn at the counter. "We're going to see everything, go everywhere, do everything," he declared. "At the ends of the roads we're going to take off with our backpacks." He hoped Mike was hearing this—he needed to be reminded—but Mike was a few feet away at one of the tables and busy talking to Marilyn's father.

Marilyn had the bluest eyes. She looked interested in what he was saying. What did she think of him?

"We call our trip the Big Wander," he told her. "I can't believe we're finally on the road after thinking about it for so long. What makes it even better, we have this uncle we haven't seen for a couple of years. . . . Nobody know's what's happened to him, and we're out to find him. Did you ever hear of Clay Jenkins, the rodeo star?"

"I guess not," Marilyn said apologetically.

"He was All-Around Cowboy in 1956. That means he was the world's best. Here, I've got a few pictures in my shirt pocket." He showed her his favorite first, Uncle Clay under a black cowboy hat with that trademark smile all over his face, standing by a fancy pickup that had his name and a bucking Brahma bull painted on the side. Then he showed her the one with Uncle Clay in all his sequins and bangles standing in front of bright lights that spelled out MADISON SQUARE GARDEN.

"That's the biggest belt buckle I ever saw."

"That's for All-Around Cowboy," Clay said proudly. "He did it all—he rode bareback broncs and saddle broncs, bulldogged steers, even rode the bulls. He hit all the big-time rodeos, like Pendleton, Cheyenne, the Calgary Stampede. . . . Wait, there's one more."

Clay took another photograph from his pocket and held it out. Uncle Clay's face didn't show very well under his black Stetson, and his chipped tooth and three-day beard made him look a little like an outlaw. He wore jeans, a long-sleeved plaid shirt, and a silk neckerchief, and he was leading a burro.

"He doesn't look the same."

"Well, it's our most recent, from two years ago. He's older—it was taken after he left the rodeo. The last we knew, he was trying to make a living as a uranium miner."

" 'The Lonesome Trail,' " she read from the border at the bottom of the picture. "Where is he now?"

"That's just it," Clay said. "We don't really know, and that's what's going to make it interesting. All we know is where he was when that picture was taken—near Grants, New Mexico, at the Bluewater uranium mill. And he was leaving there. He could be anywhere from Tucumcari to Mexican Hat." They were just names off the map, but they sure sounded good when he said them.

"Mexican Hat. Why do they call it that?"

"Because people wear sombreros a lot there, I'm pretty sure."

Clay noticed Mike's smirk, but Mike kept on talking to Marilyn's parents, telling how they'd saved up for the trip and assuring them that their mother was all in favor of it.

Before any time at all, their milk shakes were dry and they were standing outside shaking hands and saying good-bye. Clay noticed someone in the station wagon, a boy a year or so younger than Mike. "My brother," Marilyn explained. "He's not in a very good mood. I think he's just tired of our trip and being jammed in with all of us."

Awkwardly, Clay reached to shake Marilyn's hand. It wasn't anywhere to be found, but finally she produced it, which was a relief.

"Good luck finding your uncle," Marilyn was saying.

"You too," he replied, and flushed as he realized it hadn't come out right.

She chuckled, and then her family all turned for the station wagon.

"Did you get her address?" Mike asked under his breath.

Clay felt his face flushing red and his throat going tight. It was all he could do to wave as the station wagon pulled out. "What was I supposed to—"

Mike was shaking his head. "I'd swear your last name was Pigeon."

"It's not like I'll ever see her again. . . ."

"You never know, Clay, you never know. You could have written her at least."

I could have, Clay thought. Why didn't I think of that?

"You were too wound up to think," his brother said. "I saw you. You've never kissed a girl, have you?"

" 'Course I have."

"Yeah, right. That's why your face is bright red. You're the worst liar I ever saw. All good things in all good time, Clay Pigeon. Look, you're tall, you've got that dark hair, and you're handsome—the girls are going to be knocking down your door."

"Sure, Mike."

"You check the oil while I make a call, okay?"

It was time for Mike to disappear into a phone booth again and talk, talk, talk with his girlfriend, Sheila. Every day, and sometimes twice, Mike would slide into a phone booth and then afterward drive in a trance for a hundred miles. Clay had a bad feeling. He didn't even want to think about it. The Big Wander was supposed to be better than all the old days put together when they were hiking in the Cascades, swimming rivers, busting salmon and steelies, messin' around. But Mike's heart wasn't really in it.

The oil was down a quart—no surprise. At least we're on the way, Clay thought. Fifteen hundred miles from home and out in the middle of Arizona. Maybe Mike will snap out of it. The only trouble was, he'd been this way all spring, like he'd even forgotten he had a brother and the Big Wander was coming up. In the days just before the trip it was a matter of holding your breath and ducking out every time Mike seemed to be getting worked up to making a speech or something. If it hadn't been for the blowup with Sheila, Mike might've called the whole trip off.

Back on the road, Mike didn't speak for a long time, except to mutter, "In search of the 'Real West' . . ." Clay didn't want to ask him what he was getting at. As the shadows grew long and they drove through the Painted Desert, Clay could see the Real West out there, glowing and magical, beyond the billboards. Mike was missing it, but there was no budging him when he was in a funk like this.

Eventually it was starting to get dark, and KOMA was beginning to come in. KOMA would make his brother feel better. They'd never heard such a great radio station. It played all the great songs and it seemed to reach about everywhere, as if most of the country was in the neighborhood. The deejays would announce dances from Tyler,

Texas, clear up to Aberdeen, South Dakota, and from Columbia, Missouri, all across to Needles, California.

"Ricky Dare here, riding your way on the big signal coming at you from Ok-la-homa City, Ok-la-homa, playing the songs you want to hear when you want to hear 'em, and that's right now. From John in Cody, Wyoming, for Betty Ann in Casper, here's Gene Pitney and 'Only Love Can Break a Heart'. . . ."

Unfortunately for Mike, the signal faded just as the song began. Mike was in the mood for sad songs, sad love songs. Clay glanced at his brother, who was reaching for the dial and trying to get that song back. Mike was hurting, it wasn't hard to tell.

It wasn't as easy to talk to Mike as it used to be. For the last year it seemed like all his brother thought about was his girlfriend Sheila. There hadn't been time for him and Mike to do things anymore.

Now that Mike and Sheila had broken up, you couldn't just ask what had caused the big blowup. Clay felt bad for him but really was thankful it had happened and Mike had wanted to get out of town. Otherwise all those old plans for the big road trip would have been just a pipe dream. The phone call from Uncle Clay had helped too, but the call wouldn't have been enough.

I'd be mowing lawns this summer, Clay thought, and Mike would be pumping gas and hanging out with Sheila. We wouldn't be together out in the middle of the desert heading for New Mexico and points beyond, that's for sure.

Clay started to write a postcard.

"Who you writin' to?" Mike was still trying to tune KOMA back in.

"President Kennedy."

"Oh, yeah? No kiddin'? Just thought you'd stay in touch with the president?"

"Well, you know, I think he's the greatest . . . and I always kind of wanted to write to him." Clay was a little embarrassed now, but at least his brother was back poking fun again. "I figured out that we wouldn't be doing this trip if it weren't for him."

"How'd you figure that?"

"Well, I think it's because of President Kennedy that Mom got the idea about going to Guatemala for the summer, about helping other people—you know."

" 'Ask not what your country can do for you . . . ,' " Mike began, imitating the president's voice and Boston accent to perfection, " 'ask what *you* can do . . . for your country.' Is that what you mean?"

"Yeah, sort of. If she hadn't come up with such a great idea for her own summer, she might not have been so easy on us about being gone so long—you know, if we were leaving her home by herself."

"So we have the president to thank? Pretty farfetched, if you ask me."

"And just think if we find Uncle Clay! Then she'll really be proud."

Mike tried the radio dial again. "That's just a long shot, you know."

"We'll find him. I have this feeling."

Mike hooted. "You didn't even find out where he was when he called!"

"I know, I know. . . . I could hardly hear a thing. It was a bad connection. Really bad. I just couldn't think."

"Yeah, I know, you got so excited. Well, we know he was in Bluewater a couple of years ago, that's a start. Clay, you have your own unique style, I'll have to give you that."

Mike had a big grin across his face. Clay was sure that the farther Mike got away from Seattle the better he would feel. This was beginning to be just like the old days. And the whole summer was stretching out in front of them.

Clay returned the grin, brandished his ballpoint, and went to work on his postcard:

Dear President Kennedy,

My brother Mike and I are big fans of yours. My mother wanted to join the Peace Corps, but she's a teacher and couldn't be gone for two years. But this summer she went to Guatemala with a church group called Amigos.

Mike and I, we're out looking for our uncle. You may have heard of him—Clay Jenkins—used to be a famous rodeo cowboy. Keep up the good work.

Your friend,
Clay Lancaster

"I had to kind of squeeze it in," Clay said as he finished up.

"You think he can read your chicken scratch?"

"Do you think it will get to him if I just address it to the White House in Washington, D.C.?"

"Sixteen hundred Pennsylvania Avenue. I don't see why he wouldn't get it, and he ought to like that eight-foot trout lashed to the horse. Probably don't see many of those in Washington."

3

Oklahoma City was coming in strong now. It was getting dark. Mike liked to drive at night because the radio came in so much better, especially KOMA. Ricky Dare was playing "Return to Sender" and Mike was singing along. Clay hoped his brother would start looking more on the bright side of breaking up, the way Elvis seemed to in the song. Elvis was torn up and everything, but he didn't sound like he was going to *die* from it.

But wouldn't you know, the very next song was "Sheila." "Blue eyes and a ponytail" and all that. As soon as the song started, Mike was shot through the heart. Well, Sheila's eyes really were as blue as you'll ever see, and she did wear her hair in a ponytail. She did after the song came out, that is.

Clay knew not to try to talk to Mike during "Sheila," and it got even worse when Ricky Dare followed with "Breaking Up Is Hard to Do" as if he were broadcasting Mike's life story.

"I wish they'd play 'The Loco-Motion,' " Clay suggested, hoping to derail his brother's train of thought. "Or 'The Twist.' Hey, do you know why Chubby Checker named himself Chubby Checker?"

" 'Fraid not," Mike mumbled. His eyes seemed so lost in the distance Clay wondered if he'd get them into a wreck.

"His hero's Fats Domino."

"So?"

"For somebody who's planning to be a scientist . . . ," Clay teased. "Fats . . . Chubby; Domino . . . Checker. Get it?"

"So where'd you learn that? I thought you were born yesterday."

"Day *before* yesterday."

"You heard it first on KOMA and the Ricky Dare Show—here's Gene Pitney with 'The Man Who Shot Liberty Valance,' from the new movie starring John Wayne and Jimmy Stewart."

Mike was still talking, but Clay shushed him and hung on every word through the whole song. "New song, new *movie!*" he yelled when it was over.

"You sure are nuts for Westerns," Mike commented, acknowledging Clay's big moment. "Haven't you heard that Westerns are going out of style?"

"Sure," Clay scoffed. "Never happen and you know it. I wonder who the song's talking about, who was the bravest of them all? John Wayne or Jimmy Stewart? Probably John Wayne, that's what I think. I sure would like to see that movie."

"Horse operas . . ."

"Big doings Saturday night at the fabulous Black Mountain Playhouse in Red River, New Mex-i-co. Music by the Road-hogs—don't miss it! And don't forget you heard it right here on KOMA, coming your way out of Ok-la-homa City, Ok-la-homa!"

"Red River," Mike reflected. A sudden awareness came to his face and he said with a sly smile, "Maybe Marilyn will be there."

Clay felt a pang of hurt and surprise. Why was Mike going to bug him about Marilyn again?

13

"I'm not kidding, Clay! Her folks told me they were going next to Red River, New Mexico, to stay for a couple of days before they go home. They said they always go there—it's up in the mountains or something. So where's Red River? Check the map, pick up your jaw, and put on your dancin' shoes! Black Mountain Playhouse, Red River, New Mex-i-co."

"Checking . . ." Clay fumbled with the map.

"Anywhere near Gallup or Grants? Maybe Uncle Clay will turn up at the Black Mountain Playhouse, in the band or something."

"Found it. Red River's north of Santa Fe."

"Sounds good to me. Can we make it by tomorrow night?"

"I think we can do it . . . and still go over to Bluewater on the way, see if anybody there has any leads on Uncle Clay."

"On the back of the map—read me the population of Red River."

The best part was, Mike was coming out of his daze and thinking about what was ahead of him instead of what was behind. "Here it is. Five hundred fifty people."

"See? If she's not at the dance, you'll bump into her on the street."

He didn't want to talk about it. He felt too good and too sick to speak. Maybe he really would see her again!

They pulled off Route 66 somewhere near the Arizona–New Mexico state line onto a dirt track and found a little clearing for the night a quarter mile back among the yucca and cactus. The tailgate of the pickup served as their kitchen table. "What's for supper?" Mike asked enthusiastically.

"Chicken dinner," Clay beamed, and produced a tall can with a label picturing its contents.

"A whole chicken. I see. What goes with it?"

"That's it."

"You're kidding."

"It's precooked. You want to heat it up on a stick?"

"I'm hungry. Let's just eat it."

Clay was dismayed to find it looked so awful, with big globs of jellied fat adhering to it.

Mike pulled off a drumstick. "The bones have turned to rubber, like the whole thing's been soaked in formaldehyde." He ate the drumstick. "Well, I did ask you to take care of some food for the road. Clay, this is the best cold and greasy canned whole chicken I've had in my life."

Afterward they lay in their bags on their backs and watched the stars a long time without speaking. Mike wasn't going to say anything. Clay knew he must be missing Sheila really bad, going over the breakup and regretting. It was his job to keep his brother's mind off his ex-girlfriend or girlfriend or whatever she was, and on the Big Wander. "Mike," he asked tentatively, "do you think we'll really put a man on the moon before this decade is out, like President Kennedy said?"

"Possible," Mike murmured.

"Do you think we'll find Uncle Clay?"

"Possible."

"Do you think he still wears that big buckle, the one he won for being All-Around Cowboy?"

"Possible."

"Do you think you'll let me drive tomorrow?"

"*Im*-possible."

Clay smiled to himself. He loved it when things were going like this, more like they used to be before Sheila. Just him and Mike, off on their own together. "Mike"—he nudged him in the ribs—"you know that singer Don Ho?"

"Yeah."

15

"What if he named his son Westward?"

Clay couldn't see Mike's face, but he knew there had to be a smile on it.

"Or Tally or Gung," Mike suggested. "Maybe Heidi for a girl. Heidi Ho."

"How about Land? I'd like that for a name. Land Lancaster."

"Possible, but not Land Ho. Good night, Clay."

"Good night, Mike. Thanks for everything."

"I haven't done anything. Well, maybe I let you talk me into this Big Wander of yours. That was some dinner you set out. . . ."

Clay let his brother drift off, and then he balled up his jacket for a pillow and took in with deep satisfaction the faraway whistle from the Atchison, Topeka, and Santa Fe Railroad, and the sage smell of the dry desert air. It was altogether different from the deep woods scent of western Washington. He always felt hemmed in by the woods; he preferred the sea. This desert was like a dry ocean, big and open, with a big sky and shapes enchanting in the far off. It was pleasant waiting for shooting stars and listening to the cicadas drill their shrill signal into the night, half expecting a sidewinder to slither across your bedroll. And it all lay in front of him, this summer and these landscapes from another world, rolling into it with his big brother and eating out of tin cans.

4

"Fifty miles to Bluewater, New Mexico," Clay announced as Mike fished the truck key out of his pocket. "Maybe Uncle Clay's still around there somewhere."

"Tell me again about when he called," Mike said as he pulled back onto the highway. He turned off the radio, which was spitting static as always in the mornings. "Maybe you'll come up with something better than 'Restaurant Hay.' Just try to remember."

"I've been trying, believe me. The connection was terrible; at least I couldn't hear a thing. He was surprised it was me—he thought it was you. He said I sounded a lot older."

"Well, we haven't heard from him in two years."

"He asked about Mom, probably he asked to talk to Mom. I thought since I couldn't hear him, the best thing to do was to tell him all I could, so I told him how she'd just left for Guatemala."

"What else did you tell him?"

"Oh, you know, how she got all fired up about Amigos. I said she was going to be giving used eyeglasses to people with bad eyes, and all that stuff. I told him they didn't have any telephones where she was going, so he couldn't call her there. I told him she wouldn't be back until the end of August."

"But what about him? Nothing about what he's been doing? Just that he was calling from some place called 'Restaurant Hay'?"

"It only sounded like that. Mike, you wouldn't believe how hard it was to hear. It sounded like he was calling from Timbuktu."

"Come on now, you've looked over that map a hundred times. There isn't any town named that. You're going to have to try harder."

"Really, Mike, that's what it sounded like."

"Are you more sure of the 'restaurant' part or the 'hay' part?"

"The 'hay' part."

"He didn't mention the name of the state. . . ."

"Probably he did, but I didn't hear it."

"Did you ever ask him to repeat the name of the town or the state?"

Clay didn't answer.

"I just can't believe, after we hadn't heard from him for so long . . ."

Clay's stomach was in knots. Mike didn't understand, he'd had this same conversation with himself a hundred times already. If only—"Wait, Mike. I remember something else. Something about horses."

"Well, that's better. What was it all about?"

"That's all I can remember—something about horses."

"Say, that's a surprise. A guy who's been in rodeo half his life mentioning something about horses. But then again, it gives us something to go on. Every time we see somebody with a horse, we can show him one of those pictures in your pocket."

* * *

18

The foreman at the Bluewater mill told them Uncle Clay had taken off to do some uranium prospecting. "Your uncle didn't take to punching the clock and working for wages. He got himself that pack burro and started prospecting. Moved on pretty quick as I recall. He was heading for Moab, Utah. Lots of uranium discoveries up there."

Clay asked, "You're sure it was Moab?"

"He wasn't around long, but you're curious about what a man who's enjoyed some fame will do when he's out of the money. To tell you the truth, I don't think he knew what to do with himself. He was starting all over in life."

"On to Moab," Clay said cheerfully as he got back into the truck. "See, Mike? We're hot on his trail."

"Via Red River, New Mexico. Don't forget about that. What's the name of that band they keep talking about— Polly and the Wogs?"

"The Roadhogs."

"Say, Clay, did you hear the one about the horse that decided he was fed up with the same old menu out at the barn?"

"No . . . ," Clay replied suspiciously.

His brother had a huge satisfied smile on his face. "Well, he decided he'd go into town and treat himself at a fancy eatin' place. And what do you guess he ordered?"

"What?"

"Restaurant hay!"

The Studebaker's old motor wasn't hitting on all six cylinders. The truck felt like a bucking horse as they climbed into the mountains in the dark, into the pines and spruce trees and cool mountain air. One headlight was blinking in and out, but they made it to Red River, all excited because they'd been pushing for Red River most of the day and here they were.

Was she here too? Clay wondered. Was Marilyn here?

The Black Mountain Playhouse wasn't hard to find. The music had already started, and they could hear it coming from down by the river. Their momentum carried them right to the big hall made of enormous logs.

A dozen kids were waiting in line, but nobody could get in until some people inside left. "It's packed in there," Clay heard someone say. "It's because of KOMA. There's people here from all over."

They bought their tickets and waited in line. The band was playing good stuff, mostly right off the radio: "Big Girls Don't Cry," "Good Luck Charm," "Duke of Earl."

At last they were next and you could see into the dance floor. "These Roadhogs are pretty good," Mike was saying. "Hey, Clay Pigeon, there's just as many girls here as there are guys. Tonight I want to see you make your big move."

"Yeah, sure, Mike," Clay mumbled. He kept wondering if Marilyn might actually be inside.

"Okay," the guy taking tickets said. Mike went on in, and Clay looked in one hand and then the other for his ticket stub.

He checked again. Clay started to fish in his pockets when he realized what had happened to his ticket. He'd been chewing on it. He'd absentmindedly stuck it in his mouth and turned it into a wet ball, like a spitwad.

"Hey, get a move on," the guy behind him said, a guy with a greased-back ducktail.

"Really, I had one."

The ticket-taker acted like he was a giant pain but let him go over and buy another one, then let him in.

Mike was waiting just inside the dance. "What's been keeping you? Marilyn?"

Some things you just don't tell your brother. Like how could you tell him you got so excited you ate your ticket?

Mike was looking around, and then he just up and asked a girl to dance. A slow dance—"Stranger on the Shore."

Then a fast one with a different girl. Mike made it look so easy, but that was Mike.

To Clay's surprise he saw Mike thanking the girl after "Hey Baby" and coming back over. Mike didn't say anything, but it wasn't hard to tell he wasn't feeling as good as he'd been on his way to Red River now that he was here. Sheila? Clay wondered. He's missing Sheila?

Mike pointed out a girl and tried to make him go ask her to dance, but he wouldn't. Not that way, not with your big brother pushing you. And besides, as soon as he did they'd play a slow one, he was sure of it. Slow dancing was torture, plain and simple.

"I think I'll go play the pinball machines," he said.

Mike shrugged. "I'll see you around. I'm gonna go make a phone call."

Clay played the pinball machines a long time, but he wasn't any good. He couldn't concentrate. He kept watching the door. It was getting late. The dance had to be about over. The music was so loud and he felt so lonely.

When he glanced back, there she was. Marilyn. Standing just inside the door with her brother, looking out across the dance floor toward the bandstand. The Roadhogs were starting into "The Peppermint Twist." He could dance to that!

He fairly flew down the arcade and up to her and said, "Hi Marilyn." The surprise in her face was perfect. "You wanna dance?"

The music was so loud, she probably didn't even hear what he said, but she understood. In a second they were out there dancing. The Twist was so easy. You just make like you're putting out a cigarette on the floor. Lead with one leg, keep putting that cigarette out, keep your weight on that foot, then shift to the other one. Unlike with those slow dances, you never have to worry about stepping on her feet. You just keep drying the small of your back with that imaginary beach towel. Hips going all the time, forward, back, up, down . . .

21

hey, she was having a good time too, and her smile, well, she made you feel like the sun was shining on you alone.

"How did you—," she asked breathlessly when the music stopped. "Were you just coming here? That was way back in Arizona where we met you!"

"We heard about the dance on KOMA. My brother thought it'd be fun. He heard your father say you were going to Red River. We just took a chance."

She smiled. "Dad said your mother is in Guatemala for the summer. Is that true?"

"Sure is."

"What about your dad? Is he there too?"

"My father died a long time ago, in the Korean War."

"I'm sorry."

"Last dance," the band was saying, and the music began soft and slow as the lights went way down. Clay recognized the song—"Sealed with a Kiss." A slow one, way too slow! What was he going to do now!

She seemed to be waiting for him, and she was swaying a little with the music. Everyone else on the floor was starting to dance. It's now or never, he thought. His hands barely seemed to belong to him as one met her hand and the other closed behind the small of her back.

He would be safe if he barely shuffled his feet. He would get by. He thought he'd gone to heaven she was so pretty.

Clay rested his cheek in her hair. Tropical flowers. He'd never forget that scent. "I want to get your address," he whispered. "I'd like to write you about our trip."

"Sure," she said. "It would be fun to get a postcard from one of those places you mentioned."

Halfway through the song he brought her in closer and she held him tight in return. As the music was fading he glanced up and noticed, under the light by the door, her brother waiting and his brother smiling.

22

5

In Chama, New Mexico, in Durango, Colorado, and in Monticello, Utah, Mike phoned Sheila. Always he talked for a long time. Other towns along the way he'd tried, but he didn't always catch her at home. Clay was worried. How could Mike concentrate on a Big Wander in between phone calls? What was going on with Sheila? And another thing—how long would his brother's money hold out the way he was dishing out quarters? It felt like Mike was way out on a big rubber band that was about to snap him back maybe all the way to Seattle.

Finally the Studebaker backfired its way down into Moab, an oasis of bright green cottonwoods along the Colorado River. Clay's heart leaped at a glimpse of a man with whiskers and a straw hat leading a packed burro down the side of the wide main street. "Man with a burro!" Clay shouted. "It's him!"

Mike took a better look. "Too old. Uncle Clay's in his early forties, and that guy has to be in his sixties."

"But he might know him," Clay declared, and so they stopped to find out.

"Never heard of him but I can find him for you," the

man said. "Got a nose for what's lost, me and Pal both, that's the name of my friend here."

Clay was running a knuckle down the burro's gray muzzle from just below its eyes, ringed with white, to its nose, all white like the burro had stuck its face into a bag of flour. "Pal," Clay repeated.

"Likes you, I'd say," the old-timer said. "Try the insides of her ears."

Clay extended his forefinger and the burro's closest ear swiveled to meet it. "She sure has long ears."

"About three times as long as a horse's. Of course she can hear a lot better too. Her eyes, you'll notice, are set more to the side of her head—she can see all four feet as she's walking. The name's Hubcap Willie, what's yours?"

"Clay Lancaster, and this is my big brother Mike."

They shook hands, and Clay went to scratching Pal's other ear.

"You collect hubcaps," Mike said, indicating several that were sticking out of the pack, along with pots and pans.

"Sure do. Find 'em, sell 'em, anything I can get my hands on."

"You make a living doing that?" Mike looked skeptical.

"After a fashion. Hubcap Willie's been a lot of things in his life, and he's only gettin' started. Fought in the First War, owned a sheep ranch in Australia, flew for the Mexican Air Force, run cows, run whiskey, run a dude ranch, skinned cat, married seven times, owns a gold mine."

"How come he isn't mining it?" Clay asked.

"You mean, me?"

This was getting confusing. "You said 'he.'"

"Never said 'he.' Don't try to confuse me, boy. For one thing, his mine's in Mexico."

"There, you said it. You said 'his.'"

24

The old-timer scratched his head, then proceeded slowly. "Mined originally by the Indians, then by the Spanish with the Indians doing the dirty work, then by me."

"That's better," Clay said. "Now I know who we're talking about." Out of the corner of his eye he saw Mike smirking.

"Anyway, his third wife's people ran him off and it wouldn't be too healthy to go back."

You just did it again, Clay thought, but I won't mention it. "What's 'skinned cat'?"

"Drove a Caterpillar tractor in the woods—loggin' work. Don't know much, do you? Now, you boys would appreciate finding your uncle who is lost?"

"We didn't say he was lost," Mike said. "We just don't know where he is. He's the kind of guy who's always moved around a lot."

"What kind of work's he do?"

Mike shrugged. "Maybe prospecting, but who knows."

"Anything he does he's good at," Clay explained. "Uncle Clay could've been anything, that's what my mom says and she's his sister. He left home during the Great Depression when he was fourteen, the same age as me, and he did all kinds of jobs. Mostly ranch work. He always sent money home too. When he came back to Washington he worked on a salmon boat for a couple of years. He fought in the South Pacific near the end of the war, and after that he started following the rodeo circuit. Got to be a star—Clay Jenkins."

"Never heard of him. Learned rodeo in the army?" Willie asked with a grin, "or was it on the salmon boat?"

Clay liked this old guy. "He and my mom grew up on a ranch in eastern Washington—a little town called Starbuck."

"Never been there."

Clay handed the old-timer the most recent photograph,

25

the one with the burro. "Last we know of him he was prospecting for uranium."

Hubcap Willie studied the photograph a long time. "One of the Men Who Don't Fit In," he pronounced finally.

"We knew that," Mike said.

Now Hubcap Willie studied Mike awhile. "And you're a college boy."

Clay thought the old man was pretty sharp. "Mike's a whiz at math and science," he said proudly. "He's going to the California Institute of Technology in September. He might even be an astronaut."

Mike laughed, embarrassed to have his dream talked about.

"Wouldn't let them send me up in one of them tin cans," Hubcap Willie said gravely. "You know the first one to go up was a monkey."

The burro started braying.

"*Monkey*, Pal, not *donkey*."

"I thought you said she was a burro," Clay said.

Hubcap Willie eyed him suspiciously, as if he were confusing things again. "Same thing, burros and donkeys. Desert canaries. All the same animal."

"I'd go," Clay said.

"Go where?"

"Up in a rocket. To the moon."

"What for?"

"I dunno, just to go. To beat the Russians."

"Beat 'em to what?"

"I dunno," Clay said with a shrug. "Just so they don't get there first."

"So you haven't seen this man," Mike said, taking back the photograph.

"Not yet, but there's plenty of uranium prospectors in this country. Somebody will have seen him. Seek and ye shall find, College Boy."

"We've got all summer," Clay said.

"I wouldn't say that," Mike corrected him.

Clay couldn't believe what Mike had just said. It was supposed to be until they found Uncle Clay or their money ran out, whichever came first. And Mike had agreed they could work along the way to keep the money coming in, the way Uncle Clay had always done.

"Big brother here isn't as hot onto the project as little brother. Well, searches can take a considerable time. Hubcap Willie himself searched six years for his mine before he found it. But we'll see what we can do."

As Mike fired up the Studebaker, he said, "We don't need him."

"I kind of like him—and his burro."

"I think our friend's got a pound of shrapnel in his head, probably from the combat he saw in the Mexican Air Force."

At the Moab uranium mill across the muddy Colorado, a brawny fellow with a handlebar mustache remembered Uncle Clay. With a hearty laugh he said, "Uranium prospector? Not hardly. I remember a card game where he staked his Geiger counter and lost it, then said he didn't care to be digging around anyway for something that might end up in a bomb. He wasn't in town for any more than two or three weeks as I recall, before he took off."

"Took off for where?" Clay asked.

"I just can't tell you," the foreman said. "But word was he was seen in Mexican Hat a month later, leading his burro down the road."

Clay's heart jumped. He'd told Marilyn his uncle could be in Mexican Hat, and he was only making it up! "But what happened to his truck?" he asked the foreman. "He had a fancy truck with a bucking Brahma bull painted on the side."

"Funny thing—he practically gave it away here in Moab. Sold it for maybe half of what it was worth. Sold it to a kid in town who was a local hotshot in rodeo and was just starting to compete on the circuit. I'll tell you, that was one happy kid. I remember your uncle saying he was so tired of the road, he'd be happy to stick to where a burro would take him. Imagine how many hundreds of thousands of miles that man drove and how many towns he passed through in his life. I guess I'd be sick of the road too."

"Thanks," Clay said. "Thanks a lot. We'll try Mexican Hat."

"Uncle Clay could be out of the country by now," Mike said as they climbed back into the Studebaker. "He could be in Canada for all we know."

They drove up into Arches National Monument to take a look around. Mike said he needed to do some thinking and wandered off by himself. Clay took off in another direction. He'd always wanted to find some petrified wood and so he started watching the ground closely. He liked this redrock country. Everywhere you looked, domes and arches and buttes and fins and canyons, with the Colorado River cutting right through it all. It reminded him of Monument Valley, where some of his favorite Westerns were filmed. He didn't know where Monument Valley was but he sure wanted to go there some day.

A distinctive triangular shape caught his eye, lying on the sandy soil held by the occasional scrubby trees, piñon pines and junipers. Not an arrowhead. He knew a shark's tooth when he saw one and this was a shark's tooth, only it was made of a stone.

Back at the truck, Mike admired the shark's tooth only a moment. He was too preoccupied to appreciate it properly. As they drove back to Moab to look for a campground Mike didn't even speak.

The only place to camp turned out to be right next to

Hubcap Willie. Mike circled the whole campground but every other spot was taken. "That's all right," Clay said. "He won't bother us."

"That desert canary better not start singing in the middle of the night."

In the evening Clay wandered over and showed Hubcap Willie what he'd found.

"Sure enough shark's tooth," Hubcap Willie agreed. "Petrified. Trade you for it."

Clay wondered how much it might be worth. There was no telling. "Like what?"

"A fifty-six Chevy and a fifty-four Buick."

The tooth was rarer than he'd thought. Lucky day! Two cars for one fossil. He and Mike could sell both of the cars, or keep one and sell one and the truck. . . .

The old-timer fetched two hubcaps from his collection. "They're beauties."

"Oh," Clay said quietly. "No, thanks, I don't think I'll trade." He took to scratching the burro's ears. The burro sure was on the pudgy side, he noticed. Must be a big eater.

"I'll go three, but that's the best I can do."

"I kinda want to keep it." He was already thinking of who he wanted to give it to.

"Say, Pal takes a shine to you, I can see that. Of course she'd run with anybody that'd scratch the insides of her ears."

Clay fed the burro a peppermint off his palm. "Pretty good," laughed Hubcap Willie, displaying the stub of a finger on his own left hand. Clay liked the burro's huge brown eyes, the fat white belly and legs, and the thin, dark stripe that led all the way down her spine from the bristly mane to the paintbrush of a tail. "Kind of a funny marking," he said aloud.

"Sure enough. Every donkey's got it, all the way back to the one that carried Mary into Bethlehem, or so the story

29

goes. The cross of Bethlehem, they call it. Shows up really good on a gray burro like Pal. Long piece down the spine, cross member across the shoulders."

"I might like to have a burro some day. Like my uncle."

"Your uncle's no fool. A burro can carry as heavy or heavier'n a horse, did you know that?"

"Really?"

"No question. More endurance, more alert to danger, more surefooted even than a mule, and only a camel can tolerate thirst better than the burro."

"Is it hard to pack her?"

"Not once you know how. There's an art to packing right, that's for sure. You don't want an animal to be rubbed raw, even if a burro does have a tougher hide than a horse, which is why the flies don't bother 'em nearly as bad. And the load has to be perfectly balanced."

"We're going to Mexican Hat tomorrow—where my uncle went."

"In that case, I wonder if you and your brother wouldn't mind giving us a lift down there tomorrow."

"We don't have a trailer."

"Don't matter. Done it plenty of times with a pickup."

6

"The air's so dry out here, my fingertips are cracking open," Mike was saying. "Never seen anything like it."

"Mine aren't," Clay said.

"I guess that makes you a desert rat. You like the heat too, I guess."

"I don't mind it. That's what deserts are supposed to have. The good part is how it cools off every night. Every morning you're starting over."

"Yeah, the nights are okay."

Mike's nose was peeling pretty bad too, but Clay wasn't going to point it out. His brother sure burned easily with his sandy hair and fair skin. And new freckles were showing up on his forearms.

Clay took a look over his shoulder through the cab window into the bed of the pickup. Every time he glanced back it still seemed strange to see somebody there, but Hubcap Willie and the burro sure made a picture. The burro's knees were folded underneath and those long ears were standing straight up and alert. Her huge eyes, those delicate eyelashes, and that expression around her mouth and whiskers seemed to say, "I sure put up with a lot."

That brushy switch of a tail was beating a rhythm almost like Pal was counting the time of this latest trial in her life.

It hadn't been as easy to get the burro into the truck as Hubcap Willie had indicated, and Mike hadn't made it any easier saying with his eyes "I told you so" a half-dozen times at least, and then saying it out of the corner of his mouth for good measure. But now that they were rolling, if "rolling" could describe the motion of their bucking horse of a truck, you'd have to agree that hauling a load this colorful sure seemed like the kind of thing to be doing on a Big Wander. Well, Mike wouldn't agree, but that's because he was just being disagreeable this morning.

They asked around about his uncle in Mexican Hat, a tiny town perched by a suspension bridge over the San Juan River where it narrowed and entered a canyon. Upstream, lots of cottonwoods; downstream, all slickrock. At the store, the café, the gas station, nobody had ever laid eyes on the man in the photograph with the chipped tooth and the three-day beard.

Nobody here wore sombreros after all, Clay noticed. They wore cowboy hats, some straw and some felt like the Stetson his uncle favored. He'd like to get one of those himself, black with that deep middle crease.

Mexican Hat, it turned out, was named after a formation balanced high above the river on a skinny rock pedestal. He'd seen it himself on the way into town but had thought it looked exactly like a flying saucer. He hadn't mentioned the resemblance to Mike because Mike was stewing, and Mike kind of let you know when he wasn't in the mood to be jollied up with commentary like "Flying Saucer, Utah, would have made an even better postmark." Clay had seen plenty of weird town names as he scoured the map for Restaurant Hay. Truth or Consequences, New Mexico, struck him as one of the weirdest.

They were back on the road and still carrying that unusual pair of hitchhikers in the back. It was awful quiet in the cab. Back at Mexican Hat, the old-timer said he'd be pleased to ride with them just a little farther. Mike couldn't refuse him, but now he was even grouchier than before. Mike finally broke the silence, grumbling, "He said all he wanted was a ride to Mexican Hat."

A flat tire fit right into the way things were going. As Mike leaned all his weight into the tire iron, Clay reported, "We're almost back into Arizona." Mike didn't have a hat on. His forehead was burning up and dropping sweat into his eyes. "Lemme help," Clay suggested.

"Lug nuts are too tight," his brother grunted, meaning "too tight for you, but not for me," which may have been the case, but maybe not. Clay was tall, nearly as tall as Mike, and almost as strong. He could see drops of blood squeezing out of a couple of Mike's dried-out fingers. Mentioning it wouldn't change anything. Sometimes Mike just liked to suffer. Feeling worse made him feel better.

"Lucky you've gotten this far with this truck," Willie chimed in from the back of the pickup as he hovered over Pal, ready to keep the burro from standing up.

For once Mike saw things the old-timer's way. "We've got a dead dog for a motor. We might have a better chance of getting back home with your burro."

"Want to swap?" Clay suggested playfully. Then, looking around at the tall buttes and slender towers of red sandstone showing up in the desert ahead, he mused, "It feels like I've been here before."

He surveyed again the expanses of red desert studded with stranded buttes and mesas, pinnacles, towers of solid rock. "I know I've been here before," Clay said aloud, "but that can't be."

"Nope," Mike grunted, lifting the spare onto the bolts, "can't be."

"Monument Valley!" Clay declared. "It's Monument Valley."

"Last time anybody checked," Hubcap Willie agreed.

"Oh, man! *Stagecoach, Fort Apache, She Wore a Yellow Ribbon, The Searchers* . . . John Wayne country!"

"Maybe you'll get into a movie," Mike groused. He pitched the flat tire onto the burro's pack boxes and turned to inspecting his fingertips again. Clay climbed back in the cab. He wished Mike didn't feel so bad.

"No clues," Mike said as they got under way again. He was biting on his bottom lip, and that was never a good sign.

"How do you mean?"

"Uncle Clay. No leads, and you haven't located Restaurant Hay. So what are we doing out here in the middle of nowhere?"

"Just looking around I guess. Somebody will have seen him. Maybe in Monument Valley. Can you believe this! It's even more spectacular than in the movies!"

"We'll ask in Monument Valley. But you know, he really *could* be in Canada. I'm not sure you're being very realistic."

"But we have to try, Mike. We'll find him. I know we will."

"Our money's not holding out too good, you know."

"Mine is. I've got one hundred and seventy-six dollars. I could start paying for the gas—why don't you let me?"

"Yeah, and that's your life savings. I doubt if Mom would be too happy about you spending it all. And I should be making some money this summer, not spending it, even if I do have a scholarship."

"We could get jobs. Work for a while, travel for a while . . ."

Mike was working his lower lip again, even pulling on his left earlobe, the one their mother always said he was going to pull off as he was solving his most difficult math problems. "We don't know much, Clay. Maybe that wasn't even right, about him being seen in Mexican Hat."

"Sounded right to me."

"I mean, what's he to us, really. Why are we even looking for him."

Clay couldn't believe Mike had said something like that. His breath caught in his throat. Suddenly he felt like he had a fever.

"Now don't get upset," Mike said. "I want you to think about it. Let's look at the facts. How often does he call or write?"

"You know Mom says that doesn't mean anything. He just doesn't like to write letters. He's not that kind of person."

"What kind of person is he? Do we even know? Look, Clay, I don't think you see him the way he really is. How could you? You haven't even seen him since you were eleven."

"I was twelve. He took me out salmon fishing three days straight. I spent a lot of time with him—at least I used to."

"It's because you're named after him, isn't it?" Mike said. "That's what it's all about. You've built him into this larger-than-life—"

"That's not true," Clay interrupted. Why was Mike doing this? What good was it going to do?

"Maybe he's more of a misfit than a hero. Just because he was a rodeo star. . . . You know he never made much money."

"Money isn't everything. He is something special, Mike. I've always known it. Mom knows it. You used to."

"What I'm talking about is you and your heroes. John Wayne, for example. Life isn't a Western, Clay, with good guys and bad guys."

"Isn't it?"

"Maybe when you're fourteen."

"Yeah, well I'll be fifteen in December. And I like Westerns just as much because of the adventure, and the places—like Monument Valley here."

"Maybe it's because you can't remember our father. Uncle Clay isn't our father, you know. He's not even like him."

Clay's head swam. What was Mike getting at? "I've tried to remember him. How could I? I was only three when he got killed."

"He's your original hero. Shot down trying to cover some foot soldiers in a war . . ."

"I know all that. You've got people you look up to too, Mike, like President Kennedy and the astronauts—Alan Shepard, John Glenn, Gus Grissom . . . you think our father was a hero. I know you do. So what are you saying?"

"Oh, I don't know, Clay. It seemed like I had a point there somewhere. I think you're fine. I don't think you're . . . well, you're just kind of starry-eyed I guess, but that's all right. We didn't grow up like everybody else, that's all, with both a mother and a father. . . ."

Clay broke into a grin. He didn't know why, but he felt better than he thought he might, the way things were going. "For being so smart you can be kinda dumb yourself, Mike. Sure I'd like to have a father, but I wasn't going to nominate Mom's brother."

"Maybe you're right. Maybe it's a good idea to have heroes. Like President Kennedy, like John Wayne . . ."

"Like Marilyn Monroe," Clay said, and laughed. It felt good to be laughing.

Clay lingered at one of the many empty tables in the dining room at Goulding's Trading Post and looked out the windows and across to Monument Valley. The late light was bathing the monuments in a glowing golden aura like the world was ending. He was writing a letter to his mother.

36

There was only Mrs. Whitmore to clean up all the mess the tourists had left behind, and he sure felt sorry for her. She had a long way to go. "Mind if I write a few letters here?" he asked. About his mother's age, Mrs. Whitmore wore her hair tied back under a blue bandanna. "Sure," she told him. "Make yourself at home."

He could see Hubcap Willie down by the big cottonwood where Mike had parked the truck. The old-timer had a little campfire going down there, probably was cooking supper. The burro was standing by waiting for whatever came next.

Clay was telling his mother about the trading post, how different it was from the tourist traps on Route 66. How it must be a hundred years old, built out of rocks shaped one at a time into blocks—you could still see the chisel marks in them. How the ceilings were made out of logs crisscrossed by hundreds of sticks, how this very room he was writing in was where the casts of the John Ford Westerns ate their dinner every night while they were shooting the movies.

> The walls of this dining room are covered with photographs from the movies they filmed here. I'm writing under the eyes of John Wayne and Henry Fonda and Indian chiefs. I'm seeing some Navajos around the trading post. They don't look like Indians in the movies— no feathers! The men wear the same kind of stuff as Uncle Clay—it's the women who are really striking. Full skirts, long-sleeved blouses of shiny green or blue velvet, silver and turquoise jewelry all over—rings, bracelets, silver squash blossom necklaces . . ."

He set aside his pen. It didn't feel right to be writing letters when this woman was working all by herself. He was going to write to Marilyn next and send along the shark's tooth, but he could do that in the morning.

"Thanks," Mrs. Whitmore said, "I could really use the help."

He bused the dishes while she loaded the dishwasher and cleaned up in the kitchen. He'd cleaned the tables and had that letter started for Marilyn when Mrs. Whitmore came out of the kitchen offering a bowl of ice cream topped with chocolate sauce. "Never heard of a kid who didn't like ice cream," she said, and sat down across from him.

Like her husband in the trading post store, Mrs. Whitmore didn't know anything about Uncle Clay. "So you're going to travel and work your way around the West," she said, after he'd told her his whole story. She paused and said, "How'd you like to work for a while right here? We're shorthanded."

"At the trading post?"

"Right here in the dining room. Three meals a day. I already know you'll do a good job."

Clay took another look around the walls, at the photographs. Right here in this room! "What about my brother?" he asked quickly.

"We need a hand at the gas station. Fifty cents an hour for you, a dollar him. Not much, but room and board won't cost you anything."

He found Mike at the truck, gathering up their bedrolls and ground cloth. To Clay's surprise Hubcap Willie was lying down inside the cab. "I was listening to the radio and cleaning up the bed of the truck," Mike said. "He just kind of moved in to the cab. He said it was the closest thing to a bed he'd seen in a long time."

"You're going to let him sleep in there tonight? Inside the truck?"

"Yeah, I guess. He'll turn off the radio after a little while—he said he wouldn't run the battery down."

Clay smirked but he didn't say anything. His brother wasn't such a tough guy after all.

There weren't many good sleeping spots. They found one about a hundred yards away under some box elder trees and away from the glare of the trading post's night-light. Clay thought he'd kept his big news to himself about as long as he could, and spilled it. Mike wasn't as excited as he should have been. "Well, I can see you're all fired up about staying here," he said slowly, and he thought about it a long while.

"I'll try it a few days," Mike concluded guardedly. "Make back a few bucks."

Clay woke with the first desert light. He liked the time between first light and sunrise, and besides, he was too excited to go back to sleep.

A coyote trotting by with its long tail hung low stopped to look at him, cocked its head as if to wonder at him being up so early, and trotted off among the yuccas. The first streams of the sun were lighting up the monuments of Monument Valley, and the towers looked more orange than red in that early light.

Mike would sleep awhile. Clay dressed quietly and slipped away, down to the cottonwood at the edge of the arroyo where they'd left the truck and Hubcap Willie. Pal always seemed to be on her feet, and he'd been wondering if burros slept lying down or standing up. Maybe he'd find out.

It took a moment for Clay to realize as the cottonwood tree came into sight that something was missing. The burro was still there, tied to the tree and standing up. It was the rusty Studebaker that was gone. Their backpacks and their other things lay heaped in a pile, but the pickup was gone.

Hubcap Willie had left behind, for them apparently,

every bit of his gear that went with the burro. Clay found the note on Pal's pack saddle:

Dear Boys,

Hubcap Willie decided to take you up on your offer and has hereby swapped his faithful burro Pal and all of Pal's gear for your Studebaker which is ailing. Hubcap is sure you boys have got the better of the bargain but will not complain. You'll have need of hoofs to find your uncle if he really is a prospector, and Hubcap Willie will have need of wheels where he's headed. Your search for your lost uncle has reminded him of a loved one who lives far away that he has not seen for many years. Don't be concerned that you have sold an old man a bum motor because he is a crack mechanic among other things and knows his way around a wrecking yard. Be good to Pal and she will be good to you, and by all means never strike her for she is a noble soul.

Truly,
"Hubcap"

P.S. This is hereby considered a lawful bill of sale.

Clay looked around to share his amazement with someone, but there was only the burro switching her tail and looking at him with those huge, liquid brown eyes. The burro wrinkled her nose, bared her teeth, and began to bray like a lonesome freight.

"Hee-haw to you too, Pal," Clay said, and ran back with the note in his hand to tell his brother.

7

Clay waited anxiously as Mike read the note from Hubcap Willie. His brother almost seemed relieved when he finished it. Mike looked up and said, "Let's go home, Clay. Let's just go home."

"But Mike," Clay shot back, "that's not a legal bill of sale. We can show it to the police. They can stop him and we can get the truck back. Let's hurry!"

Mike was shaking his head. "It's about to break down anyway. Let Hubcap Willie buy the oil and keep it running. He says he's a crack mechanic."

"But—"

"C'mon, Clay, you said we'd swap him the truck for the burro. It's a perfect joke on us, it'll make a great story. Anyway, I'd rather go back on the train. I was thinking, we can take a bus down to Route sixty-six and then catch the train at Flagstaff. Don't you think that would be great, riding up high in that Vista Cruiser with all the windows? Great views . . ."

"What about Uncle Clay?"

"We've got absolutely nothing to go on."

"What about our jobs? What about Monument Valley?

Mike, it's only the twenty-second of June! We've only been gone a couple of weeks!"

"Two of the longest weeks of my life, I'm afraid. . . ."

Here it comes, Clay thought. *Sheila. Don't say it, Mike.*

"I miss Sheila something awful, Clay."

He knew Mike was looking at him, but Clay kept his eyes on the ground. "I thought you broke up with her."

"You know I've been talking to her. We talked again last night, a long time."

Clay hesitated. "Are you going to get married?"

Mike laughed. "Not anytime soon, I hope. We both want to go to college first. Look, I just need to get home and get back to normal, get my job back at the station or somewhere else, and start seeing her again."

He couldn't look at his brother. Probably Mike would get married a lot sooner than he said. It was too awful to think about. The next thing you knew, his brother would have kids and Mike would be somebody else and not very much his brother. It was happening right this moment—his brother was changing and leaving and it had always been the two of them.

Mike took him by the shoulders and said with a little laugh, "It's going to happen to you someday too, mark my words. Some Marilyn will come along—"

Clay laughed, but he was fighting to keep his eyes dry.

"Tell you what, Clay. Let's stay around here for a few days at least, so you can see Monument Valley and get your fill of busing dishes."

But he didn't get his fill of busing dishes. How could you, with those scenes from the movies all around you as you worked? Indians all lined up on a ridge with their battle lances, a cavalry column marching through Monument Valley, and all the while the eyes of John Wayne following you around the room . . .

Outdoors on your own time, how could you ever get your fill of Monument Valley itself or get tired of living right under those sheer red walls hundreds and hundreds of feet high? He liked everything about the place: the red soil, the twisted junipers, the prickly pear cactus, hawks sailing, ravens thrashing the air with their ragged wings. . . . He liked visiting that burro down under the cottonwood, and he liked the way Pal would snort and shake her head with her ears flapping. The ears were always going, like radar dishes swiveling around.

He bought a bale of hay for the burro, carried buckets of clean water. He talked to her and scratched her ears and thought about how strange and a little wonderful it was if even for a few days to have a burro just like his uncle had a burro.

Clay went through the gear Hubcap Willie had left behind. Mike had no interest in it, but Clay liked it because it spoke of the faraway places. Tins with traces of oats, flour, cornmeal, and rice, a couple of two-quart canteens, pots and pans and utensils, a saddle blanket, pack boxes, a tarp, even a harmonica with a fancy engraving of a steam train under the words "The Midnight Flyer."

He liked to wander among the formations early when it was cool and when the light felt rare and golden. On his third morning walk, he could sense that he was running out of time. Mike was itching to go home.

Clay was walking down a sand dune when it came to him, the inspiration, fully formed and perfect. *No reason to go home just because Mike is.* . . . He even tried it aloud. "No reason to go home just because Mike is!"

When he got to the bottom of the dune, he looked back up at it and at the sheer red cliffs behind. A smile came to his face. It had to be the exact spot from the scene in *The Searchers*! He could almost see Natalie Wood running down the dune toward him with the cruel Comanche named Scar

43

in pursuit. But the thought of taking on Scar didn't seem as appealing as pulling Marilyn Monroe out of the river.

He walked on, deep in thought. His inspiration grew into an idea and then a plan as he pictured being on his own, out here in this country he'd always dreamed about. There'd be nothing much for him at home, nothing new and different certainly. Mike would be with Sheila all the time anyway. He'd be alone in the house all summer, with Mom gone and all. In the fall Mike would be off to college. It was time he started thinking for himself and finding his own way.

"What do you say we head back tomorrow," Mike said one evening as soon as he got back from the gas station.

Clay had been preparing himself for this moment. Not like he was telling and not like he was asking either, Clay answered, "I've been thinking I've got the best summer job I could ever ask for. It's like a summer job and scout camp combined. I don't want to leave, Mike."

Mike was awfully surprised at first. "You mean, just leave you behind all by yourself?"

"That's right," Clay answered. "I'll be okay. I'll do fine."

"I'm supposed to be looking out for you," Mike said. "What would Mom think? I don't know, Clay. . . ."

"Mom would let me," Clay answered, trying his best to sound convincing. "I'm going to be fifteen in December. And besides, I'm not out here alone. The people at the trading post will keep an eye on me."

They talked into the night. Clay could see the tide was turning for him. Mike was beginning to picture it!

Finally Mike said, "I think you're right. I think there's at least a good chance Mom would go along with this, if she could see what a good setup you have here, how nice these people are. It's a great opportunity for you, and she's always been a soft touch where you're concerned."

That cinched it! "Probably you'll get homesick after a week or two anyway," Mike added. "Then you can take the bus down to the train, same as I'm doing."

In the morning, shaking hands with his brother, Clay knew this was the biggest day of his life. He couldn't keep a few tears out of his eyes. "I know this means a lot to you, Clay," Mike was saying. "I think it's going to be a good experience for you to be on your own. But seriously, take care of yourself. Don't make me regret this."

"I won't," Clay said. "Thanks, Mike. Thanks again."

"Oh yeah, and when you leave, be sure to trade the burro and the gear for as much cash as you can get."

Then his brother was getting on the bus, waving, and then sitting by the window waving as the bus pulled out. Clay was waving too and fighting back tears. He swallowed hard and watched the bus until it gradually merged with the desert's horizon and finally blinked out. His brother was gone.

Those first few days he wasn't so sure he could make it without Mike, or if he wanted to. At home, days could go by with his brother hardly even being around, but that was different. In the truck they'd been thick as thieves, and now there were thousands of miles between them and not even a trace left behind to show they'd even been on the road together.

He'd never been this far away from home, that was for sure. As he calculated that Mike must be nearing Seattle he could picture himself hopping on a bus and heading back too. Maybe Mike was right, that's what he'd do. And Guatemala seemed even farther away than it had before. Maybe he would head back home. Even if he wouldn't see much of Mike, it would be good to have him close by.

But Clay held on into the fourth day and the fifth and the sixth. He kept badgering himself to keep believing he could stay on here by himself. Maybe it was stubbornness that kept him going. He didn't want his brother to think he couldn't make it on his own.

When he felt lonely he thought of Uncle Clay leaving home at fourteen. Uncle Clay must have felt lonely too. Even when Uncle Clay got older he still felt lonely—you could see it in his eyes when he'd come to visit now and again. But you could see as well in his grin and in the way those eyes would shine as he spoke of the mountains and the deserts, that he knew life was lived best as an adventure, and he wouldn't trade his wandering, lonely way of life for any other.

Even in the clatter and commotion of mealtimes, with thirty or forty tourists all chattering at once, he'd keep glancing at the photos on the walls and lose himself in those big empty places. I still think Uncle Clay is out there, he kept telling himself. He's not in Canada. He's *out there*.

Right on Mr. Whitmore's cash register in the trading post, he posted the photograph of his uncle with the notice underneath: HAVE YOU SEEN THIS MAN? IF SO, CONTACT CLAY IN THE DINING ROOM.

A few tourists just wanted to know who the man with the burro was and all, but nobody had seen him.

With each day that he stayed Clay felt himself growing stronger. Maybe he wouldn't hop on that bus anytime soon. Maybe he could stay the whole summer as he'd thought. Maybe he would, and maybe he should.

He'd always been a hiker. When his days off came he took Pal out on long hikes through Monument Valley. No pack, just the halter and lead rope. He discovered that Pal didn't take kindly to being led; she'd plant her front feet and make you tow her like a ship on dry land. But if you walked alongside she liked it just fine. She wants to feel like we're in this together, Clay thought. More of a partner.

Clay wrote letters: to his mother, to Mike, to Marilyn. Marilyn was becoming more important to him all the time.

He found he could tell her things the way he wouldn't tell them to anyone else. He could let her know his heart, his innermost feelings. Well, not everything, but the way he felt about the desert, the red cliffs, the sunsets. And he was beginning to explain how he felt about her too. "Write me care of Goulding's Trading Post," he wrote. "I'm really looking forward to hearing from you and finding out what you thought of that shark's tooth. I've been thinking maybe a jeweler could drill a tiny hole in it and hang it on a delicate gold chain. Then you could wear it around your neck."

Along about the ninth of July, he got a new offer from Mrs. Whitmore. Would he like to go over and help out at the other, smaller trading post at Oljeto twelve miles to the west, where they needed him even more? For a week at least and maybe longer if he liked it? "It's around the back side of the mesa," she explained. "A few tourists wander through now and then, but it's the real thing, strictly trading with the Navajos. You'll be doing some of everything as opposed to just working in the dining hall here. You could learn a lot from old Weston, maybe even ride the horses."

Clay thought about it. He thought hard. It was fun being around the tourists and all the activity, but working at a remote trading post, that would be something to tell Mike about and Marilyn too. "Can I take my burro?" he asked Mrs. Whitmore.

"I don't see why not."

She found him an old Navajo man to teach him how to pack Pal right. Clay couldn't tell if Charlie Dilatsi didn't speak English or just didn't talk, but he watched closely as Charlie cinched Pal's forward and back belly cinches and adjusted the neck strap and the tail strap. When the pack boxes were packed—"panniers," Hubcap Willie had called them—the Navajo tarped Pal's load and secured it with a diamond hitch, which Clay more or less remembered from scouts.

When he was all ready he mailed a postcard to Mike, telling him he'd be over at the other trading post where there was no phone and not to worry. He could still send mail. Clay bought himself a new pair of jeans, a long-sleeved plaid shirt, and a black Stetson that he immediately creased down the middle. He looked over the cowboy boots but Mr. Whitmore said he'd probably be more comfortable in his own broken-in hiking boots. "One more thing," Clay said, and picked himself out a fancy silk neckerchief, a blue one.

"Well, you sure enough favor him," Mr. Whitmore said, with a nod to indicate the photo on the cash register.

Clay peeled loose his uncle's photograph and stuck it in his pocket. "I surely hope to," he said. He paid his money and walked out onto the porch. He felt like a new man.

All that was left to do was fill his canteens and tie his backpack to Pal's load. When he'd done that he clucked, "C'mon, Pal," and steered down the dirt road that skirts the cliffs of the big island in the sky that lay between Goulding's and Oljeto. Clay looked back, hoping there was someone to wave to. Charlie Dilatsi gave him a tiny wave, and now he could see Mrs. Whitmore up there by the dining hall waving vigorously under her blue bandanna.

It seemed as if Pal and he had been together for years. The burro seemed content to take up once more the job she was born for, and Clay spent the day feeling exactly like his uncle and picturing Uncle Clay approaching from the distance, leading his burro. He wouldn't say anything; he wouldn't shout, "It's me, Uncle Clay!" He'd let the realization come slowly into his uncle's eyes and watch that trademark grin light up his uncle's face.

A man and his wife who'd wandered away from Goulding's slowed their sedan, then stopped and asked if

48

they could take his picture. "Don't mind a bit," he said cordially, and when they took his picture he realized it was a Polaroid camera they were using. "Could I have one of those pictures?" he asked on the spur of the moment. For Marilyn! was his next thought. This is going to be perfect!

The couple was so pleased to oblige they stopped the car and got out, and as the man tore back the cover sheet Clay was able to see himself and the burro materializing right before his eyes. Just as they took the second picture, he wished he'd been tipping his hat. That would have made it even more perfect. He knew what he'd write for Marilyn on the border at the bottom of the picture: "The Lonesome Trail."

Crumbling stone buildings gave Oljeto Trading Post the appearance of a ruin. Clay liked how it was tucked against the cliffs and commanded a view out to the west as big as the country. You looked out across the broad flats of Oljeto Wash to buttes and high mesas with open sky between them, and towering over everything, the dark sloping mass of a mountain rising high and alone into the sky like a breaching whale.

Two sheep were browsing among hulks of old cars and trucks, rusted-out cookstoves and heaps of tires. Chickens were pecking along the margin of a little garden fenced with wire, poles, and rusted bedsprings. A few of them were starting into the open gravel in front of the trading post. The leaders paused as if for cover at the base of an old-fashioned gas pump, the kind with the skinny glass top Clay liked because you could actually see the gasoline and the bright-colored balls that swirled around and around with the gas moving through.

Clay paused before walking up closer and looked back across Oljeto Wash once again. At the foot of the mesa, surely, that was one of the Navajos' homes called hogans.

From this distance it looked simply like a mound of red earth.

"If this place isn't the real thing," Clay said to himself, "then the real thing doesn't exist. No billboards and baby rattlers out here, Mike."

He heard a sudden sound something like a burst of air through a tire valve, and just as quickly those chickens ran flapping and squawking back toward the garden. Clay looked up from one especially indignant hen with a stain of brown juice on her feathers, and saw for the first time an old man rocking back and forth behind the shade line on the porch.

8

Weston could spit prodigiously. Clay came to think that the old man had developed spitting into an art form. A thin old man under a straw hat with more veins on one face than Clay had ever seen, Weston spent most of the day rocking and chewing out on the porch. Every so often on the forward stroke he would spit tobacco juice in the direction of the mesa, "Hoskininni Mesa" he called it. Sometimes it seemed Weston might be trying for the mesa itself, and Clay chuckled thinking maybe he'd hit it a few times in his younger days.

Whether or not Weston had two names Clay never found out. Weston's daughter and son-in-law normally ran the place, but they had gone somewhere and Weston was minding the store more or less.

Clay settled into the chores around the place. He brought in the eggs in the mornings, tended the garden, fed the two sorrel horses, swept the store and the porch, cleaned the bathroom, cooked eggs and hamburgers for him and Weston, made change for the Navajos. Right away he posted his uncle's photograph with the caption HAVE YOU SEEN THIS MAN? on the glass countertop where people couldn't miss it.

Weston did all the dealing when it came to the Navajos' pawn. The people would come to the trading post to have their jewelry set aside for a line of credit so they could buy groceries, cloth, and hard goods, everything from nails to shovels. It seemed an awful shame to see the Navajo women take the rings right off their fingers and give them up across the counter. Even their silver squash blossom necklaces.

The good thing about Weston, you could pester him with questions and he'd never tire of elaborating on an answer. Also he'd say yes in one form or another to any question you asked him, which seemed unusual and interesting.

Maybe Weston just liked having someone around to talk to, Clay decided. The Navajos spoke barely enough English to trade, and the trader seemed to speak no Navajo at all. Quite a bit of the bartering was carried on with fingers raised for numbers. "Do they ever get their pawn back?" Clay asked.

"Of course. You can't sell it off within the time limit you agreed on, or they'd never do business with you again. If they pay what they owe by the time it's due they get their jewelry back. If not, it's gone, usually over to Goulding's."

Clay loved to ask questions about the area, especially about where the Navajos lived. "Is Hoskininni Mesa named after a person?"

"Sure is. He was the chief whose band hid out during the 1860s in that country out there—" Weston spat toward the mountain Clay had thought of as a rising whale, hitting an old galvanized bucket which gave off a convincing ring. "Kit Carson, you ever hear of him?"

"Sure."

"Kit Carson scoured the reservation at the head of the U.S. Cavalry, rounded up the Navajos, and made 'em walk to Fort Sumner, New Mexico, hundreds of miles away for most. 'The Long Walk,' they still call it today. Destroyed their cornfields and killed their stock and cut down their peach trees. Starved 'em out. Anyway, Hoskininni's band hid out in this remote country between here and Navajo Mountain and managed to live free during the years the Diné were in exile. 'Diné' is what they call themselves—it means 'the People.' "

"I never knew any of that."

"Yessir. As for Kit Carson, he wouldn't talk of that campaign in his later days, so the story goes."

"They should make a movie of the true story of Kit Carson and the Navajos and Hoskininni. It sounds better than anything you could make up."

The trader spat. "Well, they should. You know, these Navajos have dressed up to play Apaches, Cheyenne, Comanches, you name it—everything but themselves."

"What does 'Oljeto' mean, Weston?"

" 'Moonlight on Water,' I heard once."

"Where's the water?"

"Where you find it, I guess."

"Do you speak any Navajo, Weston?"

"Too lazy. Heard it's as different from our language as Chinese. That about scared me off."

"You know, I always wanted to know how to ride a horse."

"Like your uncle you were telling me all about."

"I'd never be that good, I just want to be able to ride. He and my mom grew up on horseback, she always says. I never got a chance, living in Seattle. So what I was wondering, could I ride those horses over there? Would you teach me how to saddle 'em and ride 'em and everything?"

"Naturally."

"I've got a pair of cowboy boots picked out in the store. Would you take them out of my wages?"

"Prices are high way out here. Forty-nine bucks. You'll have to stay around a while to work those off."

Forty-nine dollars! Clay thought to himself. That's over half what Mike paid for the truck!

Still, he wanted those boots.

He rode a couple hours a day, around the buttes and across the arroyos and onto the mesas, wishing his uncle could see him like this, tugging on his Stetson and riding with the rhythm of that big animal underneath him. At first he'd beaten his behind raw going against the motion of the horse, but the soreness was passing now. Where a horse couldn't take him Clay scrambled on his feet. He climbed up and into three of the ruins of the Ancient Ones, the cliff dwellers Weston said had lived here long, long before the Navajos.

He wouldn't have a complaint in the world if only he'd get a letter from Marilyn. Every day he was more sure than the last he'd get a letter or two or three forwarded from Goulding's as Mrs. Whitmore had promised.

Finally a letter came, but it was from Mike. Anyway it was a fat one. All full of expectation, Clay settled into the other rocker on the porch and broke the seal. Even if it wasn't from Marilyn, somebody out there knew he was alive.

Inside he found two letters, one from Mike and one from his mother. He read hers as fast as he could. It described all about her long automobile trip through Mexico with the other volunteers on the way to Guatemala, and it was mailed before she even got to Guatemala. "Maybe you won't even hear from me once I'm in the interior. I'll try to get mail out but the mail is notoriously slow from Latin America to the States. Take care, you guys. Make me proud."

You'd be proud of me, Mom, Clay thought. If you could only see me now!

Mike had nothing new to say. "Guess you like it out there. Nothing much going on here, same old stuff." Then it got more interesting when Mike talked about the old truck. He said how much he'd enjoyed the trip in the Studebaker, all their crazy adventures, and especially all the time they'd had to be together.

Dummy! Clay wanted to shout. We could have had all summer together!

Nothing at all about Sheila, Clay noticed, folding the letter and putting it away. But then, Mike never really told him much about her.

It sure was exciting to get mail.

"Mind if I try some chewing tobacco?" he asked Weston.

"Up to you."

With his eyes on Hoskininni Mesa, he chewed and rocked. The mesa helped get his mind off the sweet foul taste of the tobacco, especially if he kept his eyes right on that hogan at the base of the cliffs over there.

He was doing all right until he made the mistake of burping. Some of the wad slid straight down to his stomach. It wasn't long coming back up, along with breakfast. He felt sick to his stomach for the next twenty-four hours.

"I'm cured for life before I even started," he told Weston the next day.

"Yessir," the old man said. "Nasty habit."

He wrote to his brother and mother and Marilyn all about Oljeto, trading with the Navajos, learning to ride horses and all, but he left out about the chewing tobacco.

He'd been at Oljeto long enough for his earnings to pay off a boot and a half when an old Navajo couple came in early one evening and bought some groceries, mostly canned goods. The old man wore his gray hair tied up behind his head in white cotton string like his wife's. Their dark faces and hands were deeply lined, from years out in the weather, Clay guessed. Other than that he wouldn't have long remembered them; they spoke little to each other and not at all to him until they were just about leaving. The old woman had come back up to the counter to get some hard candy when her head kind of dropped down toward the countertop and all he could see was the neat way she had her hair tied up. Next thing, she'd called her husband back in and the pair of them erupted in a lively exchange. That's when Clay saw the old woman pointing to Uncle Clay's face in the picture.

Clay looked again. Her finger went from Uncle Clay's face to her own front tooth, which she now tapped a couple of times before returning her finger to the countertop and Uncle Clay's face.

"You've seen this man?" Clay asked incredulously. "That's my uncle—that's right, he's got a chipped tooth! Did you see him? Where'd you see him?"

"Yes," the old man said, happy to agree.

Weston had come inside to see what the commotion was all about. "Weston, they saw him!"

The old couple was nodding agreeably. Clay shouted, "They've seen my uncle! Find out where, when!"

The Navajos were looking from him to Weston and back, ready to be helpful if only they knew how. "They don't speak English," Weston explained.

"They said 'yes'!"

"That'll be about it. I know these people."

"Horses," the old woman said helpfully. "Horses."

"Horses!" Clay declared. "Something about horses!"

"Paiute," her husband added helpfully.

"Paiutes! That's an Indian tribe—I've heard of them. Paiute horses. My uncle must be riding Paiute horses. . . ."

The old people couldn't keep this up. They would smile apologetically and look at the floor, and then look away. Almost like they'd been cornered and had to get free, they turned and went. Clay tried to hold on to them. He ran after them keeping up a stream of questions as they stepped briskly now for their old truck. His manner only seemed to hasten their departure. He couldn't believe it, but he had to watch their truck disappear in the dust.

Clay looked back to Weston still standing on the porch. Weston hadn't seemed to be of much use at all. "You let them go!" Clay cried, all exasperated. "They know about my uncle! They've seen my uncle!"

"Now that's really something," Weston said, settling back in his rocking chair.

"You know these people? You know where they came from?"

"Why sure. Pull up a seat and I'll tell you all about it. Their name's Yazzie. They don't trade as much here as they do over at Navajo Mountain Trading Post, but I see 'em from time to time. Their grandson about your age speaks good English, and so does his dad. Too bad they weren't with the old people today."

"She said 'horses.' What did she mean?"

"She seemed to connect your uncle and horses. . . . Maybe they knew about him being in the rodeo. Can't say. But I can tell you what they meant by 'Paiute.' They were telling you where they saw him—at Paiute Creek. That's these people's sheep camp where their family spends the summer. They weren't leaving you high and dry. They wouldn't have said 'Paiute' just to say where they're from, because they know full well I already know that. They told you where they knew your uncle from, I'm sure of it."

"Then he's there now!"

"Could be, or else he passed through there some time ago."

"He's there now! Why else would they mention it! And 'horses'—maybe he has a horse now instead of only the burro. Maybe that's what they meant. So where is it, their sheep camp?"

"A little over halfway between here and Navajo Mountain. As the raven flies, maybe thirty miles."

"Can I call right now? Go over to Goulding's and call? I could talk to that boy who speaks English, or his father."

Weston laughed out loud. "That'll be the day. Not only is this the Navajo Reservation we're talking about, it's the most remote part of the reservation. Call 'em up—that's a good one."

"How close can I get on a road?"

"About right here. A couple miles closer if you went way clear around to Navajo Mountain Trading Post. I'm not sure you get the picture, son. That country's too rugged for roads—it's all up-and-down and every-which-way. People around here call all that country 'the Back of Beyond.' Nobody even lives out there year-round, only in summer. Sure makes me wonder what your uncle's doing out there. . . . Every decade or two a white man will drift in there looking for Hoskininni's lost silver mine, the one they call Pish-la-ki."

"Maybe he's found their silver and they're . . . hostile."

"*Hostile!* On the warpath you mean? That's another good one!"

"Well, where's the closest phone to their camp?"

"Navajo Mountain Trading Post."

"Then that must be where my uncle called me and my brother from, back when he called us in Seattle. But it doesn't sound anything like 'Restaurant Hay.' "

"Come again?"

"That's all right. Never mind. How long would it take me to get to Paiute Creek . . . to the sheep camp . . . if I walked and led the burro. . . . I'm a good hiker."

"You're thinking so fast your brain's going to burn up. I rode a horse, led a packhorse from here all the way to Navajo Mountain when I wasn't much older than you. . . . I suppose it would take you three or four days on foot."

"I could do it! I can read maps and all that—couldn't I do it?"

58

"I imagine you could, but doing it alone's the risky part. Nobody to help if you get into any trouble, you know what I'm talking about? What if you slipped and fell or something?"

"But you did it yourself—you've crossed through there, other people have crossed through there alone. My uncle did."

"True enough," Weston said, his gaze drifting off toward the canyons. "True enough. And I could help you get ready. Now why don't we think about something else for a while here, like fixing something to eat? We can work on this tomorrow."

It had gotten late by the time they finished supper. Looming to the west in the twilight, Navajo Mountain beckoned. Clay couldn't sleep. How could he with so many plans to make. Nothing could stop him now, he could see that. Weston would help him, he said he would.

He would have to make a plan, a way for Weston to know he had made it safely. When he got to the trading post at Navajo Mountain he could call back over to Goulding's. They could get word to Weston that he was okay. He thought about how much time to allow. If they didn't hear from him in eight days, he decided, that's when someone should come looking for him. From what Weston had said, eight days would give him time to find his uncle and to ride on in to the trading post, plenty of time. It would work out perfect.

He'd buy another two-quart canteen and that would make three. He'd take the backpack along in case the burro went lame or something. In the empty backpack he had his scout survival kit. He'd buy all the supplies he needed right here in the trading post, he'd pack that burro and throw the slickest diamond hitch this country has ever seen.

Mike, he thought. Do I tell Mike? Maybe I should go

to Goulding's in the morning, maybe I should go tonight and be there at the phone in the morning to catch him before he goes to work. I can tell him I know where Uncle Clay is and tell him to get back out here and join me.

But he won't. He won't leave Sheila, he wouldn't come all the way back out here. And then he wouldn't like the idea of me taking off by myself. Better not to tell him. If I wait I'll be able to call him from Navajo Mountain Trading Post, say hello, and then put Uncle Clay on the line. That's the way to do it. I wish I could see the look on his face!

But I can tell Marilyn. I can tell her everything.

He wrote into the night. Finally his weariness caught up with him and he brought his letter to a close:

> In a few days I'll find my uncle. It's going to be a great moment when I come walking into that sheep camp. Please write me directly at Navajo Mountain Trading Post, Navajo Mountain, Arizona. I can't imagine what's happened to your other letters—I've been wondering if you received my picture alongside Pal. I'm going to ask Weston to forward my mail to Navajo Mountain as soon as anything arrives. I'll be thinking of you. Do you know that song, "Cast Your Fate to the Wind"? Think of me out there in the Back of Beyond, Marilyn. I'll be thinking of you. The Big Wander continues!

> Lovingly,
> Clay

9

Clay woke with a start, wakened out of his fitful sleep when the back of his mind told him he wasn't just dreaming about monsters, that one was actually right next to him in the dark breathing down his neck with a wheeze and a rattle and a roar. He had no idea where he was or what was happening. It was pitch-black and something very large and not human and very much alive was right there next to him. He tore his way out of his sleeping bag, and seeing the dim form of a doorway in the darkness he scrambled for it, remembering that he was alone in the wilderness and had gone to sleep inside a long-deserted hogan.

Outside, he didn't go far. A sudden pain in his foot stopped him and reminded him he was barefoot. In the light of the crescent moon he could make out that some small something had attached itself to his foot. A cactus.

He turned around to look at the hogan's doorway and saw the silhouette of a burro's face and long ears looking out at him. "Oh, it's only you, Pal," he said into the night. "Good grief. Don't scare me like that."

He'd forgotten he even had a burro, or left her on a rope long enough so she could come inside. Well, now he knew they sometimes do sleep lying down. Clay laughed at

61

himself out loud, but the sound of his own voice being extinguished by the darkness and evoking no reply hardly reassured him. He shivered all the way through his spine. Was it the desert's night air or his own fear? He'd never felt like this when he was out with Mike.

Mike. His brother had no idea he was out here. "You'll be safe here," he remembered his brother saying when he agreed to let him stay behind at Goulding's. "Don't make me regret this."

The burro came outside the hogan and Clay ducked back in and fumbled for his flashlight. Carefully he pulled the cactus segment free of his toe. Now it was stuck to his finger. He shook it loose and it stuck to one of the poles in the hogan's cribwork roof.

Clay got back in the mummy bag and zipped it all the way up. He could turn back, he considered. It had taken so long to get packed he'd only made it around the north end of Hoskininni Mesa. He could be back at Oljeto by afternoon. He could go back to work there or even back at Goulding's, and have word sent somehow to his uncle to come visit him.

What would Weston think about him quitting? The old man had even worked on Pal's feet, which hadn't made the burro happy. Weston hadn't been sure Pal's shoes would stay on, and he said there'd be a world of bare sandstone to cross. . . .

He tried his belly, his side, his back. His wadded-up jacket felt more like a stone than a pillow.

The night air in the desert had a bite to it. Still, the cold didn't compare with the North Cascades, or even the damp woods along the coast. He had to smile thinking about all those freezing nights when he was out with Mike in the old days. Mike had told him that he'd heard you slept a lot warmer in a sleeping bag if you slept with no clothes on at all. It was hard to follow, but Mike had some explanation for the science of it. So he'd followed Mike's lead, and he'd shivered all night long—for years. He never slept at all unless in fits. It was Mike who eventually experimented with sleeping with his clothes on, and suddenly the old science was overthrown.

For a long time after that, Clay remembered, he'd slept in every layer he had until he was so bulky he couldn't roll over, until he was so warm he thought he'd roast.

Pish-la-ki, Clay thought. The name popped into his head like a magic word. Abra-ca-dabra, pish-la-ki. The lost silver mine of none other than the legendary Hoskininni. He could picture his uncle digging with a pick deep inside the mine, working only at night and by the feeble light of a headlamp. Uncle Clay might do that; treasure would appeal to him. Or perhaps the silver was already melted into bullion, and Uncle Clay had discovered its hiding place, and the Navajos have caught him with all those silver bars. Weston had laughed, but the Navajos might not think it was so funny. Maybe they had him locked up in a cage in their sheep camp . . . but then why would the old Navajos have drawn attention to his picture at Oljeto . . . that still didn't explain about horses or Restaurant Hay. . . .

Clay had almost drifted off to sleep when he heard the scampering of little feet on the dry leaves that had blown into the hogan. His flashlight revealed a cactus mouse with its outsized hind legs hopping around the dusty floor. He ushered it outside and was almost asleep again when sudden barks shattered the stillness not far away at all. He bolted upright. It wasn't but a second until the barks became yips and the yipping shifted into quavering sirens climbing higher and higher in pitch, as maybe a half-dozen coyotes harmonized like a band of lunatics and brought the hair rising on the back of his neck. Barks, yips, howls, and then only the quavering sirens wailing in the night, reminding him just how alone he was and how little he knew.

As suddenly as it had begun, their singing ended. Clay reassured himself that the coyotes wouldn't come after him. It was a good thing they thought he was so powerful. He wasn't going to tell them any different.

Almost asleep again, he thought he heard a faint whimpering outside. No, he thought, lifting his head. Just my imagination.

But as soon as he put his head back down he heard it again. This time louder, at the doorway.

A patch of white. A little ball of white. Clay flicked his flashlight on, and its beam fell on a tiny dog trembling and wanting to come in. A tiny curly-haired white dog with brown ears and brown patches over his eyes like question marks. "Come on in, little guy," he said reassuringly. "Did those coyotes scare you too? You can come in."

The little dog came in with his head almost on the ground and wagging his long tail hopefully.

Clay went to the door. No sign of any people, just the night and the stars. "Where did you come from, little guy? Did someone leave you alone out here?"

Clay stayed up talking to the dog and petting him, and listening to his whistling breath as the dog fell happily asleep. "Curly," Clay said aloud. "I'll call him Curly." He fell asleep with the dog's paw on his hand, and he woke a few hours later looking into the dog's bright black eyes, alert and friendly. Curly's tail was beating out a rhythm on the dusty floor.

He mixed up some powdered milk and made pancakes, plenty of pancakes with canned peaches he diced and added to the batter just for the occasion. Mike would have been impressed. Curly liked the pancakes just fine and ate like he was starving, which he probably was.

Pal came over and joined in, ate two or three before Clay sent her back to browsing for her own breakfast. After grazing on the sort of brush that made Clay's mouth hurt just watching, the portly burro came back over and gingerly removed and chewed up the label from the peach can. Any sort of paper she considered a delicacy.

Clay oriented his map with the biggest landmark around, the broad forested dome of Navajo Mountain rising to the west. "You just joined the Big Wander," Clay told Curly. "Lucky for you, you found me. Lucky for me I found you. You may not believe this, but I was thinking about turning tail."

The dog lay down, ran his tongue up and across his rubbery black upper lip, and placed his two front paws barely on the map.

"What do you think, Curly? Across the head of Copper Canyon—doesn't look too steep—up and through the gap between No Man's Mesa and Nakai Mesa, down into Nakai Canyon, up onto Paiute Mesa, and down into Paiute Creek to find the sheep camp. That's how Weston said to go. And that's where we meet up with Uncle Clay. Big black hat, on horseback or leading a burro. Chipped tooth . . . no, not the burro, the man. You ought to have a conversation with Hubcap Willie if you think I'm confusing. Hubcap was an old desert rat I met. Maybe that's what I'm turning into, a desert rat. What do you say, Curly? We can do it!"

The little dog barked sharply in reply.

"That's it, Curly. You and me, pardner."

10

Half an hour down the bare slopes into upper Copper Canyon, Pal's load shifted and pitched over on one side. A few more steps, and one pannier ended up practically underneath the burro. Clay's empty backpack was dragging the ground.

The burro was looking at him with undisguised disdain.

"Sorry Pal," Clay apologized. "I thought I had those belly cinches tight. I'll never do it again."

There was nothing to do but unpack and start over, and it wasn't much fun. As early as it was, the day was scorching already. Being pinned in one spot sure didn't help.

A minute after they'd started up again, Pal lay down. She was obviously having second thoughts about this expedition.

It took some mighty pulling to bring her to her feet.

A little ways farther, she lay down again.

Clay looked for something to hit her with, to make her get back up, when he remembered, "Never strike her for she is a noble soul."

"Rise, noble donkey!" Clay commanded, pulling with all his strength on the halter and lead rope. "Help me, Curly!"

The dog's high-pitched barking did seem to help. As Pal rose to her feet, the burro's lustrous eyes and droll mouth seemed to say, "Sure you know what you're doing?"

Clay pressed into the barrenlands hoping the day would produce a rain shower, but it hadn't rained since he arrived at Monument Valley and this day was starting out like all the others with the sky nothing but blue. And he'd started on the last of his two-quart canteens already. Back in Oljeto he'd thought a gallon and a half was plenty of water. In the Cascades he and Mike had carried only a quart each.

"This isn't the Cascades," he observed aloud, surveying the gravelly redlands around him and the slickrock monuments scattered here and there to the north and back to the east. "And this isn't the movies either. We'd better find some water. Nobody's going to come looking for us for seven more days."

It felt like the moisture was being sucked out of him by the minute. Now that he'd started thinking about being thirsty, his throat felt more and more parched. In the wide wastes of Copper Canyon, Clay found no water along the bottoms of the gullies. Thank goodness for my long sleeves and my hat and my trousers, he thought. You wouldn't have a chance out here without them.

"We could stand to find water anytime now, guys," he told his companions.

He wandered ahead into the heat of midday until he knew he didn't have any choice, he had to get out of the sun. At last he found a bit of an outcrop with just enough shade for him and the dog.

Clay crouched there all afternoon, moving by fractions of inches with the small piece of shade, and watched the moon set. Too bad the moon's not up in the evenings and brighter, he thought. I should be traveling when it's cool. Curly had his tongue out and was panting heavily. It was alarming to see how steadily the beads of water dropped from his tongue. The burro stood in the open with eyelids at half-mast.

When he started up again in the late afternoon, Clay thought he'd try saving Curly all those thousands of steps, and set him in the little hollow in the tarp atop Pal's load. Curly could see the advantages right away. He never even thought about jumping off.

Clay walked on as the late light erased the midday glare and brought out the true and vivid colors of Copper Canyon: blue-green, gray-blue, purple even, with a brilliant scarlet red glowing in the highest formations. "Vermilion" he'd once heard that shade of red called. He passed through the gap between No Man's Mesa and Nakai Mesa and started down into Nakai Canyon in the dusk, searching the bottoms of the gullies for water. The July day held on and the dusk lingered, but he found no water. The canyon was dry.

When darkness all but caught him he had to quit the search. "Dry camp," he announced to his companions. "The good part is, we're almost halfway to Paiute Creek. We're making good time."

Clay lifted Curly down from the burro. Faster than Clay could even register on what was happening and reach for the lead rope, Pal took off clattering down the canyon.

"No!" Clay yelled after the burro. "Pal, no, what are you doing?"

He was so angry at the burro. He scrambled after her as fast as he could. Panic ripped him as he realized how fast Pal was disappearing into the night. Pal had everything! The last bit of water, all the food, the map, the survival kit inside the backpack—everything.

"Pal!" he called as he ran. "Pal, come back!" He was running blindly toward the sound of her hoofs. Suddenly, his shin struck a rock and he was lying in pain on the hard, dry creek bottom.

It took long minutes before the pain would clear. That ball of white was licking his face. "I just hope I haven't broken my leg," he told the dog. "What if I've broken my leg?"

He was breathing hard and shaking through and through. He thought of his brother, but he'd put himself beyond Mike's help and beyond all help.

He knew the night couldn't be this cold. He was going to scare himself to death. "Calm down," he told himself. "Just calm down."

At last he could try the leg. It was going to be okay.

I'm still in bad trouble, he thought. Why'd you get so angry? Why'd you act so stupid? Settle down. Don't panic and do something even worse. What were you doing running around in the dark?

Think about the morning. Think about what you're going to do if you can't find the burro. How long can you last without water?

He sat back down and the dog nestled into his lap.

You're going to have to find water, Clay told himself. Where can you find it for sure? Think of the map. You studied it enough you should know it by heart.

The San Juan River. All these canyons between Oljeto and Navajo Mountain flow north into the San Juan River, on its way to join the Colorado River. The San Juan's the river you and Mike crossed upstream on that suspension bridge at Mexican Hat.

If only Hubcap Willie had got off at Mexican Hat the way he was supposed to, he never would have ended up taking the truck. None of this would have happened.

Why didn't I just go home with Mike?

What if I can't find the burro?

Clay had all night to try to fight back his fear, to regret and shiver and think. If the days are long the nights have to be short, he kept telling himself. I'll drink my fill at the river, then head back for Oljeto when the sun's starting down. Jog in the dusk, go slowly by starlight if possible. Jog through dawn into the morning.

He couldn't sleep for shivering, and he couldn't talk the fear out of his bones. The night went on and on and on.

At first light Clay started moving down the bottom of the canyon. At least he was moving. He scanned the slopes on the sides so he wouldn't pass by Pal accidentally.

All slickrock, the canyon bottom showed no hoofprints. He could only hope Pal had come this way, hadn't somehow doubled back. At any rate he was closing some of the distance between himself and the San Juan River before the sun started broiling again. Why hadn't he thought more about how hot it would be? It had all seemed so simple back in Oljeto.

He stopped to look at a curious structure on the left-hand side, a stairway of sorts leading from the canyon bottom up to the first ledge. It was made of piled-up rocks and a couple of bleached juniper logs. It hadn't been used in some time, but he thought it must have been built for burros or mules or horses.

He walked briskly now. He had to get to the river as soon as he could. How many miles?

Down the canyon, droppings. A pile of droppings on the slickrock. Pal droppings, fresh ones! A pile of dung never looked so beautiful.

At first he thought he'd heard a raven, but he listened again. A frog croaking, wasn't it? The brown question marks above Curly's eyes rose as he listened also, to the intermittent and eerily amplified croaking of a single frog. Clay broke into a run. Two bends down the canyon he spied a long line of greenery on the left side, about man-high on a ledge. Grasses and ferns grew above the water-stained slickrock. "Water!" he yelled to Curly.

70

The seam dripped water all along that ledge. He could drink it one drop at a time if he had to. Along the canyon's slickrock floor it didn't run deep enough that you could collect it.

Still running, he turned a corner and found his burro, fully packed, standing beside a pothole the size of a bathtub with water flowing in and out of it. Pal was browsing on a patch of grass that grew in a sandy spot, and she had a long red wildflower between her lips. Her tail was switching and her long ears swiveling. Those lustrous brown eyes and white eyebrows seemed to be saying, "Welcome to paradise. Where have you been?"

Clay grabbed her lead rope, then threw himself down on the slickrock and began to drink. Looking into the pothole, he could see diving beetles, the kind with one oar on either side. They were stroking their way down toward the bottom. Pal's face was reflected in the water—a beautiful sight. He felt so thankful. The water sure tasted good. Curly was lapping away right next to him.

Clay took an extra wrap on that lead rope as he stood up. From here on out he would never let it go unless Pal was tied or hobbled. He began to scratch the insides of the burro's ears the way she liked. "So you lost confidence in me, is that what happened? Well thanks for finding the water, Pal."

He found an alcove for the heat of the day, a room-size shady spot under a roof of stone. He unpacked the burro and opened some Vienna sausages, broke out some crackers. "Turn back or go ahead?" he asked the dog. Then he spread out the map again. He already knew the answer.

11

It was starting to cloud up, and Clay was free to come out into the open. He began to think he might be able to climb out of Nakai Canyon this day. He returned to the spring and drank again, then filled his canteens. Barely breaking the surface, Pal put her lips to the water and drank. Clay had never seen such a dainty drinker. "Let's take a bath before we go," he told his companions.

"Mighty nice," he said, settling into the cool water. "All the comforts of home." He inspected the shin with the bad bruise. It was sure enough ugly, but the swelling was going down.

Curly came close, and Clay reached out for him. The tiny dog's nails dug for traction on the rock. "Come on in, Curly. Hey, you hardly weigh anything. C'mon, you could use a cool-down."

He placed Curly in a shallow spot like a shelf in the tub. Curly stood still, wet up to his neck, and the brown patches above his eyes seemed to be asking forlornly, "Why are you doing this to me?" Clay scratched him behind his ears and along his back, then lifted him back onto the slickrock. With his white fur plastered against his sides and his tail so long and skinny, he looked more like a rat than

72

anything. Clay couldn't help laughing. "I guessed you were some kind of a poodle-cross. Now I know, what with!"

It wasn't hard to see he'd robbed the little dog's self-respect, and as soon as Curly was done shaking himself out, Clay apologized. It took some coaxing but at last the dog came to the edge of the pool and give Clay's face a few licks. The heat of the desert quickly restored his curls and his dignity.

In an hour's time Clay was standing once again at the horse ladder he'd discovered in the morning. Scanning the cliffs, he traced a route up through the ledges and onto Paiute Mesa. He hauled rocks and stacked them to make the ramp passable once again. Before he started up he thought to fold up his map and stick it in his shirt pocket along with his compass. Clay fished his survival kit out of the backpack and stuck it in his other shirt pocket. "Just in case," he said aloud. After he'd slung one of his canteens around his neck, he was ready. "And Curly, I don't think you should ride until we get to the top. I don't want you to slide off—there's a lot of cliffs up there."

Pal scaled the horse ladder without hesitation and it was a marvelous thing to see. Then the burro began clawing her way up through the ledges with the confidence of a mountain goat.

Here and there they paused to rest. The clouds were boiling up right out of the turquoise sky, monumentally tall, and were starting to turn dark. "They might mean business," Clay said. "I'm glad we aren't way down there on the bottom of the canyon."

Thunder began to rumble inside the clouds and the wind began to blow. After all the relentlessly hot days he'd seen since he first came to Monument Valley, it was pleasant to feel the wind on his cheek and to listen to thunder, to enjoy shade out in the open and watch the clouds begin to spill rain in tall columns. Even if the rain did separate into streamers and dry up before it hit the ground, it made a welcome sight and he'd take dry rain any day he could get it.

When at last Clay reached the top and the flat expanse of Paiute Mesa, he was pleased to find it grassy and sprinkled with piñon pines and junipers. Closer than ever, Navajo Mountain commanded a good piece of the sky, close enough he could make out individual trees along its skyline. Tall timber grew up there, and he could see why: the rain up there was falling wet instead of dry.

Pal deserved all the grazing she wanted, and it looked for now like she intended to eat up the whole mesa top. He fastened her hobbles exactly the way Weston had shown him, and let her graze. She couldn't go far. Then he threw himself down on the rimrock and took a good rest with Curly by his side.

I'm getting close now, he thought. All I have to do is cross the mesa and drop into Paiute Creek. I'm a long way from Seattle, that's for sure, and practically shouting distance from Uncle Clay. "Make me proud," his mother had written. That's exactly what I'm going to do, he thought.

When he woke from his nap the sun was dropping low and casting glory all around. On the far side of Nakai Canyon and tucked under the rimrock, a golden two-room ruin of the Ancient Ones caught his eye. In the eastern sky, like colossal Portuguese-men-of-war, boiling white and black thunderheads trailed streamers of evaporating rain lit up in pinks and oranges and reds, golds and lavenders and violets. Shafts of light pierced the lowest layers and illuminated the domes and towers of the redlands below. The mesas were glowing vividly purple.

The whole world seemed to drop off in front of him. He could see in the distance the shadow-casting buttes of Monument Valley and far, far beyond, a dark mountain range to the southeast. To the northeast the San Juan River ran in a winding green strip toward Mexican Hat. Set back from the river above a bulwark of tall cliffs, a forested plateau rose above the canyon of the San Juan and pitched up to mountains so high that a patch of snow still lingered above timberline.

All of it glowing and shifting and changing in a bath of colors—no two moments were the same and each, it seemed, would make a memory for a lifetime. This is why I've come, he thought. More than anything else, this is why.

If only I had someone to share it with.

Under way, walking into the evening, he let his mind drift. Pal stopped to graze where she found it to her liking and Clay didn't care to hurry her along, although he did keep a death grip on her lead rope. He was thinking of all the things he had saved up to tell Marilyn the next time he wrote. As he walked into the gathering dusk he could almost see her. Well, he couldn't remember her face exactly, only her hair. In fact he couldn't remember her face at all and that bothered him. If he tried harder it would come back.

Suddenly though, he recalled her perfume. He could smell those intoxicating flowers as vividly as if she were walking alongside him. It was easy to picture himself taking her in his arms. As he walked alongside the burro, he saw himself doing just that. He would take her in his arms and then he would kiss her. How perfect everything would be if Marilyn were with him right now.

A great horned owl hooted in the moonlight two, three, four times, and then after a pause, four times again. Clay asked the little dog, riding the pack and bobbing at eye-level alongside, "What's he saying, Curly? You can almost make it out. There, I've got it. 'You, you-oo, you, you . . . Love you, you-oo, you, you.' "

75

He found himself crossing slickrock terraces rolling like ocean waves. Before long the slickrock was cratered with deep potholes, and in the deeper ones he found several feet of standing water. Not far away stood an old shelter made of poles and roofed with tree branches. A sheep camp! Surely, a sign of the main camp! He must be getting close!

Next to the shelter Clay found a small corral made of poles and he dragged Pal in there, very much against her wishes. Then he cooked up a big can of pork and beans and fried up some biscuits. Tomorrow would be the day! After supper he visited the corral and Pal swiveled one ear forward, then the other to have them scratched. While he scratched an ear, Clay was trying to pick out a tune on the Midnight Flyer—"Cast Your Fate to the Wind."

Evidently Pal didn't think the performance up to her standards. Hubcap Willie had probably been a virtuoso harmonica player "among other things." The burro took Clay's neckerchief by her teeth and took a step back. Clay felt himself losing his balance and took the harmonica in his mouth, bracing himself with both hands against the fence. He was eyeball-to-eyeball with Pal, and he thought he saw a glint in the burro's eye. "Okay, Pal," he said, the words turning into notes through the harmonica, "you can turn me loose now."

The burro tugged a degree harder, and for the longest time Clay was suspended there, with one leg back in the air for balance like a ballet dancer. Finally Pal tugged a fraction more, and Clay felt the corral giving, and then giving way altogether as he fell down in a clatter of falling poles. The whole side of the corral was on the ground. "Okay, Pal, you win," he said, as he dusted himself off. "Let's not keep you in here tonight after all."

• • •

76

Bound for Paiute Creek in the morning, Clay could feel his strength and his confidence in his muscles and his bones. It felt like he was taking ten-foot strides.

At the bottom of the creek he was faced with a decision. Turn up the canyon toward the plateau where it originated, or turn down the canyon toward the San Juan? Weston hadn't known where exactly to find the camp; he hadn't been in Paiute Creek for over fifty years.

To the river, Clay decided at last. The sheep must need water. The creekbed was dry. So where could you water sheep better than at a river?

The canyon soon widened out to a half mile or more, and here and there the water popped up from underground and flowed awhile on the streambed before disappearing in the gravels again. He sighted four hogans up ahead in the sandy flats below the cliffs and his heart began to drum wildly. For some reason he started singing "The Loco-Motion." That didn't seem right after a minute, and so he switched to "The Man Who Shot Liberty Valance."

Unfortunately the hogans were abandoned, and seemingly long ago. A shade-break no longer provided shade, and a few logs on the ground in a ring barely resembled a corral.

He could hear the river before he could see it, and he knew he must be approaching the sheep camp and the big moment with Uncle Clay.

Every step brought him closer to . . . disappointment, as it turned out. No sheep camp, no uncle, only a boulder field where the canyon dumped into the river, and the rapid roaring where the river spilled over the boulders.

"Well, guys," Clay announced. "Nobody here. Stick with me, Wrong Turn Lancaster."

He tied Pal up to a driftwood log, then unpacked her. Close to the river would be a good place to camp for the night. When he was done with the work, he stripped and walked out onto the sand beach. His toes felt good in the sand. Then he waded out into the river and swam with powerful strokes, playing in the sandy brown San Juan like an otter. Curly was barking all the while on the beach. "Perfect temperature!" Clay shouted. "Come on in, Curly!"

As Clay pulled on his clothes it occurred to him that there just might be fish in those sandy waters. Catfish maybe. "Fresh dinner tonight!" he shouted. "I'm a pretty good fisherman," he confided to the dog and the burro. "Well, not *pretty* good, I mean *awfully* good. You should see the salmon and steelhead I've caught in my day.

"You may be wondering where I've been keeping my fishing pole. Well, an ace fisherman like me doesn't need one. I'm pretty handy with a hand line, and I just happen to have some fifteen-pound-test, hooks, and sinkers in my survival kit right here in my pocket.

"I'm sure you won't mind waiting a few minutes, Pal, while I catch us some supper. No comment? I bet you can't even hear me over that rapid. We're not talking about a can of beans, guys, we're talking about fresh fish. Doesn't that sound good?"

The dog seemed enthusiastic but the burro was baffled.

"Come to think of it, Pal, you don't look like a big fish eater."

From his supplies Clay broke out a long, rock-hard hunk of wine-soaked salami and sawed off a piece. It was his mother's ceremonial gift to him and Mike, for their big trip, as she left for Guatemala. She'd presented them with one as they set out on backpack trips for as long as he could remember, and they'd always joked over who was going to have to carry the thing, it was so heavy. "Bait," he explained to Curly, and sawed off a second hunk for himself, a third for Curly. "Don't want to eat too much of this stuff, now—you might get drunk on it."

For a long time Clay waited on the alert for a strike, but as the tall canyon walls started to provide shade, he thought he deserved a nap and he lay down on the beach.

He thought it might be fun—he'd never tried it before—to tie the line off to a big toe, and then just make himself comfortable and doze off, letting his big toe warn him if the salami found any takers. He was thinking about what a great fisherman his uncle was, and what a strong swimmer too. They were fishing from a canoe once out at Goose Lake when his uncle suddenly stripped down to his skivvies. "What're you doing?" he'd asked his uncle.

"I want to see if I can nab that big turtle over there basking on that log," Uncle Clay had said.

"How come?"

"I just thought it might be interesting."

"You won't get within fifty feet before he slides into the water, and they're great swimmers. You know how they are."

"I know," his uncle had said as he lowered himself over the side of the canoe. "That's what'll make it interesting."

Clay started to doze off. The sand sure felt good. He hadn't known his body was so sore. The roar of the rapid seemed so restful as his memory drifted him back to Goose Lake. He could remember his uncle swimming so slowly toward that log, with only his nostrils stuck up into the air like a turtle himself, he'd begun to wonder if Uncle Clay had a chance. Maybe he'd get within thirty feet. . . . And now he pictured his uncle submerging with fifty feet anyway yet to swim before the log, and then he didn't surface for what seemed too long a time, until finally Uncle Clay burst out of the water like a dolphin with arms. The turtle splashed into the water out of his reach and then Uncle Clay kicked and dived after it. He stayed under until he surfaced with a victory cry and held up that big turtle with both hands. The way that shout exploded from his lungs, you could have heard it from clear across the lake. . . .

It was late afternoon when the alarm on his toe—something tugging hard—brought him out of a dream, a sweet dream in which Marilyn was trying on his Stetson just for fun. What a combination the black hat made with her blond hair. For a second as he woke up, he could almost remember her face but then it slipped away.

Anyway he had a fish on the line and there's nothing in the world quite like having a fish on the line. There's a current running through the line that connects you in that moment to everything that's beautiful and mysterious and wonderful. In this case the current was running into him through his toe.

Clay took the line in his hand and gave it a couple of wraps. No time now to free his toe—he had a *big* fish on. Up and down the beach and out onto a sandbar he fought it, trying his best to ignore the fact that he had a piece of fishing line connecting his hand and his toe.

Working the fish up and down the sandbar, he was having a hard time trying to stay on his feet. That piece of line kept tripping him up, and twice he fell down in the water. But he'd seen the prize: a big silvery fish almost like a salmon, but with a smaller head and the fins different. Once he was onto a big fish, there was nothing in the world but him and the fish and victory or defeat. Clay could feel the world blurring away at the edges. There was only him and the fish in all the world and the current of the world was running through him.

Behind him, Curly was barking. Curly must be pretty excited about the fish too, Clay thought. Pal was snorting loudly. Even Pal was inspired by the battle. It isn't easy to give and retrieve line when your hand is the fishing reel and the line's cramping your palm and cutting your fingers.

Now's the most critical time, he thought. He's in the shallows and I haven't got a net.

Twice Clay tried to wade in after the big fish to get close enough to grab it. But when the fish saw him coming it was off to the races. At last Clay saw no other way than to pull on the line hard enough to drag the fish into shallow water, and so that's what he did. The big fish was coming onto the shallows. Clay thought he'd won the day when he heard that sickening *ping*, the distinctive sound he'd heard too many times in his life before with salmon or steelies on the line, the distinctive sound of fishing line under high tension snapping.

Seeing his long-fought prize heading for deeper water, Clay splashed in after it hoping to grab the fish somehow. But he forgot all about the length of line connecting his hand and his toe. He fell flat on his face in the river.

As he sat up, he replaced his hat on his head and turned around toward the shore. That's when he discovered two Navajos, a man and a boy, dark-skinned and dark-eyed, mounted on spotted horses right there on the shore and just looking at him. No expression at all, unless there was a trace of amusement around their lips and eyes; it was hard to tell.

Curly was looking from Clay to the Navajos and back, and wagging his tail ever so faintly.

Clay was sitting in the river with only his head and shoulders out of the water. He knew somehow that they had been watching him for a long time. The man was big and barrel-chested, his face broad and heavily lined under a flat-brimmed, tall black Stetson. Hammered nickels ringed his hat and large silver conchos belted his waist, prominent against his vermilion shirt with the tails worn long. Large silver bracelets studded with turquoise adorned both wrists.

Clay couldn't believe he'd had an audience for the worst fishing episode in his entire life.

Everything in the man's appearance and demeanor spoke authority, and for an instant Clay was afraid that the man was hostile. But the glint of humor in the man now grew and spread across the broad face as the man said in English, "You horsed him."

Now father and son, as he took them to be, broke out laughing, and Clay was laughing with them. He stood up and water streamed from his clothing.

Hatless, the Navajo boy wore a red headband and a string of red coral beads around his neck. His shaggy hair spilled over the back of his collar. The boy's smile flashed as he said, "We were wondering why you have your fishing line tied from your hand to your toe."

Clay shrugged and smiled back, and said, "Oh, just to make it interesting."

Suddenly the boy became greatly animated. He pointed in Clay's direction with his lips, then spoke rapidly to his father in Navajo. Among the boy's words, Clay picked out these two: "Hosteen Clay."

12

" 'Hosteen Clay'?" Clay's heart was pounding fast. "Did you say 'Clay'? I've come a long way, and I'm looking for my uncle—Clay Jenkins."

He walked up onto the sand and reached to pat Curly, whose tail spoke happiness at having Clay back on solid ground.

"We know your uncle," the boy said proudly. "You sort of talk like him, same neckerchief, same hat. You're Clay Lancaster."

"You know my name?"

"Your uncle spoke of you often," the man said. "And you have a brother Mike."

"Yes, but he's not with me, he went back home. . . ."

For a moment both Clay and the two Navajos fell silent, each trying to put together the pieces.

"Are you from the Yazzie family? I met an old couple in Oljeto. . . ."

"My grandparents went there," the boy acknowledged. "They aren't back yet. My name is Russell, my father's name is Sam."

Clay noticed the silver work in the horses' bridles. He'd never seen the like of it or of the splendid spotted horses.

"Your horses are really something. I've never seen such beautiful horses."

"Yes," the boy said. "*Hozhoni*—beautiful. They're gifts of your uncle."

"Really? Your grandparents were trying to tell me something about Uncle Clay and horses!"

"There's much to tell," Sam Yazzie said with great seriousness, and even a touch of what may have been sadness.

"Is my uncle's with you right now? I mean, back at your camp? I want to see him as soon as I can."

"No, he's no longer at our camp. He's across two rivers," Sam Yazzie replied.

"He's all right?"

"We see him again on the twenty-seventh of July."

"Nine more days," Russell Yazzie said. "I've been counting."

"Why the twenty-seventh? Where's he coming from? Where will you see him?"

"Let's make a camp here," Sam Yazzie said. "It's too far to return tonight. And there's some things you should know before you meet your uncle."

"Can I go with you when you go to meet him?"

"That would be a good thing."

It didn't concern the Navajos that they had no overnight gear. They would stay close to the fire, Russell said. They'd spent nights out before, it wouldn't bother them.

Clay wondered what was troubling Sam Yazzie, if there was something bad he wasn't telling. Russell's father had left them after briefly speaking to his son in Navajo, and his face seemed clouded with concern. Clay began laying out his stores, thinking about what he might offer his guests to eat. "Chili con carne . . ." he was thinking aloud. Suddenly there was a big commotion and Clay looked up to see

Pal crow-hopping around and making a big spectacle of herself.

"What's she doing?" Clay exclaimed, all alarmed. He jumped up, ran over and grabbed the tie rope, freeing one of her legs which was caught.

"Oh, I've seen that happen before," Russell said with a smile. "She was scratching her chin with one of her hind feet and it got caught in the rope."

Clay hobbled Pal so she could get around a little and graze. Sam Yazzie was down by the river assembling three long forked sticks, green willows he'd cut along the river, into a conical frame.

Clay asked, "What's he doing?"

"Building a sweat hogan," Russell replied. "He wants to . . . to purify himself before he tells you the things he needs to tell you."

"Is it that bad?"

Now the boy's face clouded. "It's very difficult for Navajo people to talk of certain things . . . to talk of people who have . . . but my father believes you need to know these things. If he prepares himself in the right way, it will be all right."

"Uncle Clay's okay, isn't he? What's happened to him?"

"He's all right. My father will explain everything. He won't eat tonight, and we won't speak to him until he's all finished with the sweat hogan."

As Clay and Russell were collecting firewood and getting the fire started, Clay watched Sam Yazzie lean upright sticks against his frame and then slabs of juniper bark. He was leaving a doorway facing upriver, to the east, chanting as he worked.

Clay might not have been able to hear the chanting over the roar of the rapid, but the wind would shift and carry the man's high-pitched singing their way, riding on a rhythm so regular and monotonous the song would have seemed to be sung to the accompaniment of a drum. Clay had never heard anything like this singing. It reminded him a little of the coyote sounds he had heard in the night.

Russell was mixing up some cornmeal for corn bread. "Wait until you get to the summer hogan," he said. "We'll have lots of frybread."

"I'd like that. I haven't had any bread since Oljeto except some biscuits I fried up."

Russell added a little more water. "This corn bread isn't as good as frybread, but it'll be good with your chili."

"A trader told me I should have some cornmeal, but I didn't know what to do with it." Clay was happy to have someone to talk to who talked back.

Russell greased Clay's deep frying pan and set it on the coals to heat up. "I'm glad you're going to stay with us. Everyone back at the summer hogan is going to be excited to see you. We'll have plenty to eat. . . . Everyone will be happy to see the second Clay. Everyone will want to hear the story of how you came searching for your uncle."

Russell spooned the batter into the pan and covered it with a metal pie plate. He spread most of the coals out of the way with a stick, then started the corn bread baking on the thin layer that remained. Picking up a coal at a time, he used two twigs like chopsticks to cover the lid with coals.

"Did my uncle live with you at your sheep camp? When?"

"Last summer . . . it was a happy time for everyone."

"But not this summer? He doesn't live with you anymore?"

Russell didn't say.

It wasn't long before Clay could smell the corn bread. He rummaged for his honey. The bread was done and so was the chili.

"What's it about, what your father is singing?" he asked Russell as they ate. "Is it a ceremony or something?"

"It's not really a ceremony," Russell answered. "It's his own way of preparing himself. What he's singing right now, it's about *Bik'é hozhoni*, the trail of beauty. This is what he's saying:

Beauty before me, with it I wander.
Beauty behind me, with it I wander.
Beauty below me, with it I wander.
Beauty above me, with it I wander.
Beauty all around me, with it I wander.
On the beautiful trail I am, with it I wander."

"That's what I feel like, Russell," Clay said, "being out in these canyons."

"Then it's your song too."

"Do you like peaches?" Clay asked him.

"I love peaches."

"Then let's open two cans for dessert. Hey, I'm sure lucky I found you. I mean, I'm sure lucky you found me. And that you speak such good English too. I couldn't talk to your grandparents at all. I mean, I don't know any Navajo. . . ."

"Oh, I go to a boarding school. . . . They only let you speak English there. At home everybody speaks in our own language. When Hosteen Clay was here my father got to use his English again. My father was in the marines in World War Two—he spoke English all the time then, except when he was a code talker."

"What does that mean—a code talker?"

"There were about four hundred of them," Russell said proudly. "All over the Pacific. The Navajo code talkers. If the enemy ever cracks your code, they know all about your biggest secrets for all the landings and battles and everything. But no matter how hard the Japanese tried, they could never crack the code made from the Navajo language."

"I never heard about that before! That's really something, that your dad was one of them."

"He was at Iwo Jima and Guadalcanal, lots of different battles."

"Uncle Clay was in the Pacific too, and so was President Kennedy."

"I know. *PT 109!* The Japanese sank his PT boat and he had to swim through the flames."

"Maybe Uncle Clay and your dad and President Kennedy all met each other in the war, only they didn't even know it. . . . What does that word mean, *Hosteen?*"

"Like 'honored.' It's usually for older men like grandfathers."

"Where is your school?"

"Oh, about a hundred miles from our winter home near Navajo Mountain."

"You're kidding! How do you get home?"

"We don't, me and my brothers and sisters. Only at Christmas, and a week in the spring. We live at the school. That's what a boarding school is," he explained. "You live there."

"That's terrible! That must be really hard!"

Russell shrugged. "Sometimes it is hard, especially at first, especially for the little kids. But that's the way it is. Summer's a lot better," he said, indicating the canyon walls or the river or all of it with a twist of his lips.

They built up the fire. In the outwash of the canyon, where the dry creek met the rapid, they gathered stones to be heated in the fire. Russell wanted round river rocks for his father's sweat hogan. Sandstone explodes suddenly and can throw little slivers like razors, he explained.

It was getting dark, but Clay could see that Sam Yazzie was packing the outside of the sweat lodge with mud now and sealing up the cracks.

Back at the campfire, they dropped the rocks in the fire and added still more fuel. Sparks were flying into the night and joining the stars.

His new friend was squatting comfortably back on his haunches but not quite touching the ground. Only his feet touched the ground. Clay could do that too, and now both of them sat that way with their hands on top of their knees.

"What are the two rivers?" Clay asked. "Uncle Clay's across two rivers, your father said."

"The San Juan here—we call it Old Age River—and the Colorado. We'll meet him where the Escalante River joins the Colorado, and help him move the horses across."

"Horses?"

"He's going to be bringing some more wild horses out of the Escalante country and across the river like he's done before."

"Wild horses! Is that what your grandparents meant by 'horses'?"

Russell nodded. "My horse and my father's—they were wild horses. Mustangs. Hosteen Clay brought them across late last summer. My father will tell you how all those things happened."

Something was turning in the back of Clay's mind, demanding to be remembered. "Es-ca-lan-te," he repeated. "You said Es-ca-lan-te."

"It's the name of the river and also the town where the Mormons live, up the river somewhere, in Utah."

"That's it! Restaurant Hay! Escalante! My uncle called us from there, and I got the name all mixed up!"

Russell laughed hard at that. "You thought the name of the town was Restaurant Hay? That's a good one. We'll have to tell that to my father."

The stones were glowing red in the fire. "They're ready," Russell announced. Carrying the glowing red stones on two poles they held together between them, Clay and Russell walked in the darkness to the sweat hogan. Then the boys poked and pushed the hot rocks into the hole Russell's father had made in the wet sand in the floor's center.

They returned to the campfire and let it burn low now. The night air was pleasant and they didn't really need the fire for heat. After a time Clay realized he was hearing the muffled sound of chanting from inside the hogan. His eyes must have asked the question because Russell began to explain. "He's singing the Sweat Bath Song now. It's an old story. It tells how First Man put down the first sweat hogan at the edge of the hole where the people came up from the world before this one. 'Everlasting and peaceful, he put it down there, the Son of the She-Dark.' That's what the sweat hogan's called—it's really dark in there too."

A little later Clay heard a sound like a stone plunging into the river. "What was that?"

"My father. Now he's bathing in the river. It's so hot in there, it feels really good when you jump in the river."

"Have you done it before?"

"Sure. Hosteen Clay liked it a lot. If you want, we can go in there. My father is finished."

"I will if Uncle Clay did."

Clay peeled off his clothes and followed Russell inside. The stones were still glowing faintly. "You were right about how dark it is in here," Clay whispered. Russell reached out and closed the door tight. "Still pretty hot too," he whispered.

"It must have been really hot when your father came in here at first."

Clay heard the hiss of steam as Russell sprinkled water from a canteen onto the stones. Instantly, a blast engulfed both of them and he ducked his head to avoid it. "Wow," he said. "That's really hot."

"You like it okay?"

Moisture was gathering all over Clay's arms, his legs, his hair—all over. He didn't know if it was steam or sweat or both. "I like it," he said.

Russell sprinkled some more water on the stones, and another blast washed over them.

Just when Clay thought he couldn't stand it anymore, Russell parted the flap and they both went outside. The moon hadn't risen over the canyon of the San Juan yet, but he could see his friend's profile by starlight. He waded knee-deep after Russell, then plunged in alongside him.

It felt cool and cleansing and . . . purifying. Clay got out and stood on the shore. He felt lighter than air. Suddenly dizzy, he sat down in the sand. The dizziness passed as quickly as it had come. He thought he had never felt better than he did right now.

Clay could feel Curly's wet nose on his arm, and he reached out to hug the little dog close. Now it was time to dress and to rejoin Russell's father by the campfire. Now it was time to learn what it was Sam Yazzie was so reluctant to tell.

13

"Three of our horses ran off the year before . . ." Russell's father began. The big Navajo man looked only into the fire. He cleared his throat, then continued.

"We knew they'd be spooky and it would be hard to catch them. It was early in the summer, just after we'd come to the summer hogan with the sheep. The yucca was still blooming. Three of us, we searched for four days in all these canyons. We were about to give up. Then we came across your uncle. He rode an Appaloosa horse with two burros behind.

"We were surprised to find a *biligaana*—a white man—in such a place. One of us joked that he must be looking for Pish-la-ki, a silver mine only white men believe in. He had no digging tools, we found out later, only things a man needs to live.

"I asked if he had seen any horses. He knew where they were, he had seen them. He led us to them. That's when we found out how much he knew about handling horses. The People are good horse wranglers from way back. Navajo people raided for horses a long time ago, we traded for horses, horses are in our blood as you say. But your uncle had his own way of gathering up horses. No one had seen anything like it.

"We invited him to come to the summer hogan and he came along with us. We only found out much later that he was a big rodeo star. Some people at the trading post recognized him and told us he used to be in all the big rodeos, that he was 'All-Around Cowboy.' Hosteen Clay had never told us that himself, and he lived with us the whole summer.

"All the kids liked him and would follow him around in a pack. The old people liked him, everyone liked him. The first time my sister—"

Sam Yazzie paused and looked straight down at the ground. It seemed to Clay almost as if Russell's father had seen something. Quickly the man looked back into the fire and continued, by force of will it seemed. "The first time my sister saw him, she liked him. I saw it, I was there. I knew her feelings. She hadn't married—no one could arrange a husband for her. She was a strong woman. But when she first saw this man it was different.

"Everyone could see that Hosteen Clay had deep feelings for her the first time he saw her. He didn't speak to her for three days, he was so shy.

"I told my mother not to speak to him again because he would be her son-in-law. She said she didn't need to be told, she already knew it.

"He hoed with us in the cornfield and in the bean field. He rode out with the sheep and kept them company every day. He worked on the stone corral where the stones had fallen down. He wanted to learn how to make silver, and I began to teach him. He wanted to know the Navajo words too. He wanted to learn everything, but quietly.

"Often we would talk about horses. He learned that we like the spotted ponies the best, the pintos. We told him that the best horses were the old mustangs, the wild ponies. They weren't big but they could run all day and never slipped and fell even in country like this. From way back, Indian people especially liked to catch the painted mustangs and breed them for their colors.

"Hosteen Clay wondered if there were any mustangs left on the reservation. We said no, just broomtails like ours that ran off. Maybe there are still mustangs in the Escalante Mountains in Utah, we said. Across the San Juan River and across the Colorado. We told him that the People used to trade with the Mormons in that country ever since way back. Jewelry and blankets for sheep and horses. Sometimes the People traded for those mustangs. But nobody had been over there since before the war.

"About this same time he was asking me about how Navajo people are married. I knew his heart before he told me that he wished to marry my sister, of course. He told me he had never married, he had no children. Now he wanted to be married to my sister for the rest of his life—how should he go about it properly?

"I asked him if he wanted to take her away and marry her in a church. He said no, he wanted to marry her here, in the Navajo way if that was possible. I told him that he would need someone to speak for him who was not of her family, a friend or relation of his. The go-between would suggest the marriage and propose the dowry, jewelry or horses usually.

"Pretty soon he asked me how to find the crossings on the San Juan and the Colorado. I knew what he wanted to do. 'There might not be any mustangs left over there,' I told him. 'There's only one way to find out,' he answered. I let him go. It was the kind of idea that made him happy. Before he left my sister saw him stacking rocks up high in the corral, higher than they'd ever been before. She kidded him about if he thought we had flying sheep, to make a pen that high. I never told her, but I think when he left the next day and said he would be back, she knew he'd be bringing horses for her father.

"Two weeks later he returned with these two horses you've seen today. No one had seen ponies as beautiful as these. He ran them right into the corral. No one pointed out that he had delivered the dowry before the go-between asked if it might be accepted.

"Along with the horses he also brought his go-between, a cowboy who helped him wrangle the horses across the rivers. The cowboy suggested the match to my father, who accepted the horses and set the date for seventeen days later, the first of September. The cowboy returned to the Escalante country.

"We built a new hogan for Hosteen Clay and my sister to be married in and to live in. I asked my sister if she thought her new husband would stay and live among us, or if they would leave sometime and go somewhere else. She said he was happy here and had said he didn't care to live anywhere else, but if he changed his mind one day it wouldn't matter to her.

"It troubled him that he couldn't help build the hogan. We laughed and told him to go out and watch the sheep. It was only a summer hogan anyway—a brush shelter. He could help when it came time to build a hogan of wood and earth at the winter place near Navajo Mountain.

"When the day came he was married in the Navajo way. He entered the hogan first, passed around the south side, and seated himself at the rear of the hogan facing the door which is east. Bringing the basket of boiled cornmeal, the bride entered with her family and took her place next to him on his right. I myself was the master of ceremonies and it was a happy day for me. The groom was my friend and the bride was my sister. Everyone could tell they would be together from that day into old age. I put the water jug in front of my sister and handed her the gourd ladle. I poured water into it and asked her to pour the water onto his hands. When he had washed his hands, he then poured the water onto hers.

"I brought out my bag of corn pollen and sprinkled pollen over the basket from east to west, and from north to south. I proceeded to do everything as it should have been done. The bride and the groom ate from the boiled corn-meal and the pollen in the correct places, in the correct order. When they were finished I instructed everyone to begin eating the wedding feast.

"They stayed in their hogan for four nights and four days, as is expected.

"For a month all was beautiful and peaceful. Then Hosteen Clay suggested that he and his wife would return to Escalante to buy several more mustangs for themselves, from the man Barlow who had sold him the others. I told him I would go along, my son as well, so that both of us could cross the Colorado and see that Escalante country as my father had, and trade with the Mormons as he and his father had. I made new silver—rings, bracelets—and brought some of my old silver too.

"We forded the rivers. It was autumn and they were low, but not so low the horses didn't have to swim. We climbed up through the tall Hole-in-the-Rock where the Mormons had made their wagon road down to the Colorado long ago. I had heard of these places but never seen them. On top it was beautiful, all rock up there.

"My sister was feeling sick, but we didn't know it until we'd ridden half the way from the river to Escalante. She had a bad pain in her stomach, and it kept getting worse. It was so far back home we knew we had to keep riding toward Escalante because it was closer.

"We got to the corral at the head of Coyote Canyon where Hosteen Clay had bought the mustangs before from the man named Barlow. This time there weren't only two in the corral, there were thirty or more. They were being loaded into cattle trailers, all crazy, fighting, screaming, breaking everything including their own bones. Two of them were destroyed right there.

"That's when we learned what was going on, from one of the cowboys. This man Barlow was bringing the horses out of the mountains and keeping them for a while at his corral at Coyote Canyon until the slaughterhouse sent trucks for them. We learned that the horses were being made into food for dogs and chickens, and turned into fertilizer. This man Barlow held back only the spotted ones because he knew people would pay well for them.

"Hosteen Clay kept his anger over these horses inside. He was concerned for his wife, to get her to a doctor as fast as he could. The cattle trucks left with the wild horses. Three pintos were left behind in the corral. We weren't going to buy or trade for them now—my sister was in bad pain. Barlow's cowboys were driving off fast with their pickup trucks and horse trailers. Hosteen Clay told Barlow he had to have a ride for his wife to get to the doctor. Barlow was the only one left. I could see he didn't like one of his kind being with us, worse that he was married to one of us.

"Hosteen Clay said he was afraid his wife might have appendicitis. Barlow laughed and said she probably had indigestion from eating too much frybread. He said he wasn't taking any squaw to the doctor. He just drove off and left us.

"We tried to ride on to Escalante. No more trucks came. It was too great a distance. My sister died in the night. Hosteen Clay took her away in the morning and buried her himself. When he came back he said he had buried his heart. He returned with us to *Diné Bikéyah*—Navajoland—but it wasn't long before he went away again.

"We didn't hear from him all winter. In the spring he wrote a letter and said he wasn't going to let Barlow take the last horses out of the mountains to be slaughtered.

"He rounded them up himself. He ran them down the canyons of the Escalante River, pushed them all the way down to the Colorado as he had hoped. We were there to help him swim them across the Grey Mesa where no one lives and where Barlow would never get them. We brought a few across the San Juan for ourselves.

"Nine days from now he'll run another bunch down the canyons of the Escalante. They could be the last mustangs in all that country. We'll be there to meet him. He won't know his nephew will be with us. That should bring some joy once again into his heart.

"That is all," Sam Yazzie concluded.

Clay saw the man glance in his direction, then look away. "Life is for the living," Sam Yazzie said. "Let's speak no more of the dead."

14

They feasted him. Clay squatted on the hard-packed dirt floor inside one of the shelters topped and sided with cut branches, and he feasted on frybread and mutton ribs and coffee. He'd never liked coffee before. He'd always said to his mother, "Who'd want to drink bean juice?" But when Russell's gray-haired grandmother, the old woman he'd encountered at Oljeto, made a pouring motion with the pot and glanced his way hopefully, he nodded "Yes, please."

The coffee was good. Maybe because it was brewed on an open fire, he thought. Russell's mother forked a new piece of frybread from the hot oil and gave it to him, smiling. The frybread tasted especially delicious with the coffee. They were pleased with his appetite. The kids wanted to make sure he was getting enough ribs. Yes, please, I'll have some more.

Clay's eye was drawn to the weaving on the loom behind Russell's mother. A blanket of dazzling color and complexity was nearing completion. How could she make that design, and make it right out of her head? And they thought he was something special. What had he ever done?

He was welcome here. He could feel it in all their faces, from the smallest kids to the old people. But who were all these people? Relatives, somehow. Russell tried to explain but it was hard to follow. They didn't call each other by their names. It was always something like, "My brother who is the son of my mother's youngest sister." They were two families of all the generations joined together, he'd figured out that much.

Many of them couldn't speak English, including Russell's mother. It didn't matter. They made him feel welcome. He was their second Clay. Everyone knew his sadness on learning of his uncle's great loss. It was theirs as well. No one mentioned his uncle or the woman from among them who'd fallen in love, married, and died.

In the evening Curly was attempting to help the sheep-dogs keep the flock in line as they blatted and funneled their way into the stone corral for the night. The children were all laughing at Curly's shrill barking, the way he ran back and forth not really knowing what to do but looking back to Clay all the while for approval. "What kind of sheep are those?" Clay asked his friend, as he pointed out one cluster with horns and especially long fur.

Russell laughed. "Those kind of sheep are called goats." The other kids were laughing too, and it didn't take a minute before the story was on its way to everyone in camp.

Clay went to sleep happy. He felt a great contentment. And tomorrow was all arranged. Russell would make the trip to the trading post with him, one day there and one day back. They'd go on horseback and take Pal to carry their supplies. He was looking forward to pulling on his cowboy boots again. He'd make his phone calls; his brother would be astonished at all the news. And Weston would be glad to hear he didn't have to come looking for him. Even better, he'd get his mail. He could see it now, a stack of letters from Marilyn. How many? Six? Eight? He could almost make out her handwriting, he could almost make out her face. . . .

100

* * *

"Got two," the trader said. The man wore red suspenders and had an oversized face, puffy like dough.

"There must be more than that."

"No, there's only two. One from a Mike Lancaster and one from a Marilyn Blanchford."

Thank goodness, Clay thought. At least there's *one* from her. A letter from Marilyn!

"This one here sure smells good," the trader teased, holding up a pink envelope. "This one from the Marilyn . . ."

Indeed it did. Clay could smell her perfume just as plain as if she were present.

The trader handed the letters over slowly, just to tantalize him.

Clay was blushing, he knew it. He wanted to get out of there and he wanted to read her letter as fast as he could. Russell was waiting outside on the bench. His eyes seemed to ask if Clay had good news. Clay didn't know yet. He sat down on the far end of the bench and tore open the envelope. The shark's tooth fell out of the envelope into his hand.

The blood pounded in his temples. He could barely breathe.

Dear Clay,

When I gave you my address in Red River, I thought you were going to send me a postcard. I hardly even know you, and here you're writing me these long letters.

Clay had a bad feeling in the pit of his stomach. Suddenly he felt weak all over.

Russell left the porch, taking a polite walk over to the horses.

You think about a lot of things, that's kind of interesting. But you get carried away. Boy do you get carried

101

away. "I think of you under these same stars," and all that—"Love," "Lovingly," and so on—it's really embarrassing. You obviously don't care about making a big fool of yourself. My parents are kind of worried about this and my mother thinks you're some kind of weirdo. And that shark's tooth! There are lots of things I'd rather wear around my neck than a shark's tooth. So while you're out there in the "Back of Beyond," GET LOST! And don't write me any more letters, please.

Sincerely,
Marilyn Blanchford

Now he was suffocating. Yes, what a fool he was, what a complete fool! All those things he'd said to her. He'd told her everything! "I think of you under these same stars. . . ." He'd said that! He'd said a lot of things. He'd never felt this awful. He'd never felt this stupid. He'd never felt this . . .

Clay called Goulding's with the message for Weston, and then he called home. Of course Mike wasn't there. Mike would be at the gas station. He called information, he dialed the station number, Mike answered. His brother was on the line. It seemed so strange, and didn't feel anything like he'd expected.

"Mike," he said, "this is Clay. I'm calling from the Navajo Mountain Trading Post."

"You're at some other trading post again? I thought you were at Oljeto."

"Well I'm here now."

"Did you get my letter?"

"Yeah. . . . They sent it over here. I forgot to open it."

"Whaddaya mean, 'forgot'?"

102

"I mean, I'll read it in a minute. I just got it. Any big news?"

"Well, no, but—"

"Look, Mike, I'm living with some Navajos that Uncle Clay lived with last summer, in fact he got married to a Navajo last summer and she died and we're going to be riding across the San Juan and the Colorado soon to meet him—he's bringing some wild horses across—and if you hurry you can get here in time to join us."

"Hey, slow down there, Clay, let's take it from the top."

Clay almost ran short of quarters trying to explain it all. Mike was having a hard time taking it all in, he seemed so far away. He was sorry about their uncle, but after it was all hashed out Mike couldn't come out to meet up with him. His job, and wanting to be with Sheila: nothing had changed. In fact he tried to talk Clay into coming home. Mike didn't really understand at all. "You can always meet him later, now that you know he's okay."

"No chance, Mike," Clay said. "Not when I'm this close."

"You sure are a persistent cuss," Mike said slowly. "I'll give you that. I don't like the part about how you took off on your own between these two trading posts. I still think you should come home. At least promise me you won't do anything else stupid, you hear?"

"Sure, Mike."

"So when are you coming home? It's already the twenty-first of July."

"After I've spent some time with Uncle Clay, Mike." Remembering it wasn't his brother he wanted to kick, he added, "Think of us on the twenty-seventh—that's when we're going to meet up. He doesn't know I'll be there."

"Still got the burro?"

"Sure, I've got her right here. I have a little dog too. His name's Curly—I'm going to bring him home with me."

"Just so you don't show up with Pal. I wrote Mom about what's going on but of course I don't know if she got the letter. Still haven't got any more letters from her. Hey, I saw *The Man Who Shot Liberty Valance*—have you seen it? It's good, real good."

"I haven't thought much about the movies lately."

"Hey, have you heard anything from that Marilyn you met in Red River?"

He hated lying. It made him feel awful. "Nah. . . ," he said.

Well, how could he feel any more awful?

He got out of there as fast as he could. Away from that trading post and back on toward the sheep camp. He rode alongside Russell without speaking. With a flick of the wrist he tossed the shark's tooth aside. His mind was on fire, it was burning up. How could she do that? How could he have written those things? What was he thinking? What did he know? About girls, nothing. It was hopeless.

They made a camp while it was still a little light. Pal proceeded to roll around on her back and take a dust bath.

Curly came and licked his face. He pushed the dog away.

Pal stepped in a tin can and got her hoof caught. Now she was hopping around on three legs again. Russell smiled, but Clay didn't see what was funny.

"The moon's starting to grow," Russell said meaningfully. "We meet him when it's half full. Not too many days now."

Clay knew what Russell was getting at, a much happier day was coming. But he said, "I don't see why they want to go to the moon anyway. There's no air up there, there's not even much gravity. You couldn't even stay attached to the ground without big old weights in your boots, and you'd have to wear a big old suit with tubes and stuff like a scuba diver."

"I guess so," Russell said.

"It's just to beat the Russians anyway. On the moon by the end of the decade and all that stuff. Maybe we won't even be alive by 1970—that's eight years off. Maybe we'll all get blown up with atomic bombs. Do you ever think of that?"

"Not much . . ."

"My brother says the Russians and us came this close last summer when the East Germans were building the Berlin Wall."

Clay realized that the thumb and first finger he'd held up were touching. He was getting carried away. His friend had his head down and was digging a little hole with his boot heel. Why was he making Russell feel bad?

"I used to worry about it a lot," Clay continued, trying to explain himself, and much more softly now. "They're always talking about whether you should have a bomb shelter. Some people have them. This one family on our block has one. Do Navajos have bomb shelters?"

"Not that I ever heard of."

"I don't think we're really going to have an atomic war. But it's scary."

"I know. We learned about it at school. We practiced getting under our desks in case there was an air raid."

"We did that too. Didn't you wonder what good that was going to do? I got my hair stuck once in some gum under there."

Russell chuckled, and then he said, "I remember once, everybody was real quiet and I couldn't help it, I said *Ka-Boom!* real loud. But the teacher didn't appreciate it."

Then they both were laughing. It felt good to be laughing again.

Clay was glad to be back in the sheep camp, glad he wasn't alone right now. Working alongside Russell, he hoed in those corn and bean fields with a vengeance. He helped to harvest squash and melons, and he rode with Russell every day on horseback to accompany the sheep. They were being called twins, to everyone's amusement. When had he ever had a better friend?

Each day it seemed they were giving him something. He'd admired Sam Yazzie's hatband of nickels, and now his Stetson was decked out the same way, with buffalo nickels he'd seen Russell's father shape over a conical mould. The silver parade of buffaloes looked sharp against the black felt. At his wrist he wore a bracelet Sam Yazzie had made, with three large turquoise stones set in silver. Around his neck he wore a strand of red coral just like Russell's. "I can't take all this," he said each time, yet each time he could see how pleased his friends were in the giving.

One evening the kids made a campfire and he played the scratchiest "Oh Susannah" imaginable on the Midnight Flyer. Then Russell tried the harmonica and taught all the dogs to sing along to certain chords that would set them off. The kids laughed especially hard when Clay's tiny white dog laid his brown ears back and sang. "Elvis," suggested one of the kids, and that's what they called Curly after that.

The next night everyone in the camp came together around the campfire. Russell's grandfather was drumming monotonously, and he and the men were singing their wild and eerie songs. Many of the boys were chanting too and dancing in the firelight. Russell was among them, shaking a gourd rattle to the beat of the drum. Thinking he'd add another instrument, Clay joined in and produced some unusual notes on the Midnight Flyer. Then he tried to chant along with the singers, which the Navajos found the funniest thing in the world with the possible exception of his dancing. Whenever he'd fall out of rhythm, or stumble as he did a number of times, the Navajos had to hold their sides they were laughing so hard. Tears were falling from the women's and the old people's eyes.

He was beginning to heal. The hurt would stay, but the scar was forming over the wound. Maybe he would always be this way. Maybe he would never be able to make his heart known to a girl. For him it was different than it was for Mike, and much harder. He'd always known it was going to be hard. It would have to be a miracle, like saving a girl from a raging river and her falling in love with you.

Then came the morning for him to leave with Russell and the men and to cross those two rivers. Pal was all packed. Curly was already settled in his perch and ready to go. Sam Yazzie had said that Pal wouldn't be too happy about crossing any rivers. Burros hate any water that's more than ankle deep, he said. But when he saw how much it meant to Clay, he said, "She'll swim when we don't give her any choice."

"Besides," Clay added. "I might need to go on to Escalante with Uncle Clay. He might be going back there."

Here was Russell, all ready for the journey, dark eyes shining as ever. He was mounted on a chestnut mare and trailing a packhorse. "Where's that painted pony of yours?" Clay asked him.

Russell's mother appeared in all her quiet beauty. Her full skirt was a deep blue, with a braid stitched near the bottom to match her shining green blouse. Around her shoulders she wore a colorful fringed blanket, and from her neck hung many strands of fine turquoise beads. She was leading Russell's spotted pony, adorned as always with

107

the silver bridle but displaying this morning a bright new saddle blanket with distinctive geometric patterns and bright colors.

Russell dismounted, and his mother handed the reins of the spotted horse to Russell. Clay would never cease to marvel at this horse's beauty. Mostly white, it had a golden mane and reddish brown spots along its spine, red stockings, red marks too on the front of its face and chest.

"This kind of horse is called a Medicine Hat," Russell said almost bashfully. Clay could see Russell's grandparents looking on from a little break between the stunted junipers. "Good war horse," Russell added with a laugh. "Some tribes say these markings are good luck because they look like a war bonnet and shield."

Clay didn't understand why Russell was telling him these things right now. The little kids were quiet, and looking back and forth between their brother and his friend.

Russell transferred the reins to Clay's hand. He glanced ever so slightly at Clay, and then he looked away as he said, "This horse is one of the two your uncle first brought from across the Colorado, to arrange his marriage. You'll look good on this horse going to meet your uncle. I want you to keep this horse."

Clay wanted to say right out, This is too great a gift. Almost twenty pairs of dark eyes were waiting now, looking away in their fashion but watching him still. He knew it was their custom also not to say "thank you" at every turn. Their dignity and pride did not allow it. But for great occasions and with great humility the word could be used. "*Kehey,*" Clay said, his voice breaking with the depth of his feelings.

His time at the summer hogan had come to an end. It was time to leave the sheep camp and to cross two rivers.

15

They waited on the banks of the Colorado. On the designated day, the twenty-seventh of July, they waited, gazing all the while across the river at the narrow canyon mouth of the Escalante, watching for Clay Jenkins and wild horses.

Clay waited with Russell and his father and four others as the half-moon rode across the daytime sky. He waited with them into the night until the moon set behind the canyon walls and darkness fell, obscuring the mouth of the Escalante River.

Clay hoped they wouldn't give up and leave. Maybe something had held Uncle Clay up, maybe he was just late.

He needn't have worried about the Navajos giving up. They were much better at waiting than he was. Together they watched through the next day, through the heat and the endless minutes and hours. It seemed his companions didn't even need to talk to pass the time. The river rolled by and lapped gently at the sandstone. The swallows over the river twisted, dipped, and climbed endlessly, those violet-green acrobats. Sometimes they skimmed the surface—for bugs or a drink of water? He kept wondering what had happened to his uncle, and worrying.

It occurred to him, he'd never once heard the name of

Sam Yazzie's sister, the woman his uncle had married. When he asked Russell, it was obvious how uncomfortable he'd made his friend. "It's not good to speak the name of someone who's dead," Russell whispered.

They waited a second night and he watched the slow passage of the waxing moon with his friend. No figure appeared at the mouth of the Escalante other than a coyote who came to the riverbank, then turned around and splashed back into the shadows up the shallow bed of the river. "It's good we've come to see this place again," Sam Yazzie said. "Next year there'll be no coyote here and no crossing."

"But why not?" Clay asked. "Why wouldn't there be a crossing?"

"Didn't you know? They've been building a big dam down the Colorado for years now. It's almost done. Next spring, they say, the water will back up into all these canyons. All these hundreds of tall canyons of the Colorado and the San Juan too. Even Paiute Creek—it's all going to be underwater."

"How far up these cliffs right here?"

Russell's father pointed almost straight up. "Way up there, they say. Only the tops of these canyons will be left. They say they're going to call it Lake Powell."

In the morning, after they had waited as long as they could, Clay knew what he would do. When Sam Yazzie said it was time to return to the sheep camp, Clay said, "I'm going on to Escalante, if I can get across. I came this far."

They transferred Pal's boxes to a packhorse, as they had for the crossing of the San Juan. It would be hard enough for the burro. They didn't want her loaded down with gear.

Russell's mother's brother led the way across, trailing the packhorse.

Sam Yazzie followed with Pal's lead rope snubbed around

his saddle horn. Clay and Russell and two others pushed forward in a tight ring and forced the burro into the coffee-and-cream-colored Colorado.

It was shallow at first, and the burro tolerated being driven. She had no choice. Then Sam Yazzie's horse was swimming. Clay saw the whites of Pal's eyes roll as the burro brayed in terror—her legs had suddenly lost the bottom too.

Clay's own spotted horse was swimming now. Curly's little head and ears were poking out of Clay's shirt, and his black eyes were looking all around. One of Clay's feet lost a stirrup but he clung tight with his legs, and clutched the mustang's flaxen mane with one hand.

Once on the far shore, Clay set to repacking the burro. Taking his leave wasn't going to be easy. He stowed everything away but the harmonica.

"The third canyon on the left side leads up to the top," Sam Yazzie said. "I remember it's got a cliff ruin in it. Maybe you won't want to go all the way up the river to get to Escalante. You could go out a side canyon."

"Just think, I'll be with Uncle Clay in a couple days!" Clay said.

Everyone stood around nodding their agreement, but it seemed none of them would speak now that the parting was so close. He brought the harmonica out of his back pocket and gave it to Russell. "I hope you can learn how to play this thing," he said. "I'm sure I was never going to."

"*Kehey*," Russell said.

"You teach those dogs of yours to sing a tune."

Clay mounted the spotted pony and snubbed Pal's lead rope around his saddle horn. "On a beautiful horse I wander," he said. "With my dog Curly I wander. Toward my uncle I wander. Saying good-bye to my friends I wander."

"Your horse's ears are made of round corn," Sam Yazzi answered, speaking in a chanting rhythm.

"Your horse's ears are made of stars.
Your horse's head is made of mixed waters.
Your horse's teeth are made of white shell.
The long rainbow is in his mouth for a bridle.
With it you guide him."

"Come back one day," Russell called as Clay rode away.
"I promise," Clay said over his shoulder.

He wound his way up the canyon of the Escalante at the feet of its overtowering red cliffs, up its gentle streambed of sand between the swath of bright green willows on its banks. Pal didn't mind the water now, it was so shallow. And it ran delightfully clear.

It was cool in the morning shadows. It was peaceful. Never in his life had Clay seen the like of these sheer red walls cut as if with a knife. He realized with a pang, he would never have the chance to share them with Mike. Next spring, water would be rising up these walls.

On some of the banks there were bright patches of clover. At every bend in the canyon, he let the mustang and the burro browse to relieve their hunger.

The canyon walls allowed him only a slice of the sky. All through the morning the slice remained a hard, bright blue. When the sun cleared the canyon rim high above, it didn't shine for long. Tall thunderheads were boiling up in what little of the sky he could see, and they were turning dark.

Faster than he would have thought possible, the wind was blowing hard and those clouds were growing positively black.

Clay urged the horse forward and felt the resistance from Pal as the rope went taut. "Let's get a move on, Pal," he said anxiously. "You remember what Weston said about being caught in the bottom of a canyon at a time like this."

He started eyeing the sides of the canyons for refuge. Nothing as far as he could see. He couldn't remember a safe place behind him. Fifty miles of this canyon lay in front of him with side canyons coming in left and right. It came to mind how Sam Yazzie had described the world on top that these canyons drained: solid rock. This isn't the Northwest, he told himself. No forest, no soil to hold the water back like a sponge. What would a flash flood look like roaring down this canyon?

Instantly, he could imagine one. Hung up high on a talus slope that fanned out from the base of the cliffs, a long white log was perched. Formerly a cottonwood tree, he realized, stripped of its branches and bleached out by the sun. Left there by ebbing floodwater. At exactly the same level, on the other side of the canyon and ahead, other logs testified to the same conclusion: this canyon could rage in a flash flood, and when it did, anything walking up its bed would be flushed out into the Colorado on a high-speed jet.

Clay passed the second canyon on his left. It might lead him up and out, but probably not. These canyons were so monumentally deep and narrow, most of them would likely cascade down to the Escalante in a series of pour-offs.

The wind blew harder still. The burro's ears were swiveling faster than Clay had ever seen them, and Curly there in the little hollow on top of the load was yawning with anxiety.

"Let's keep movin'," Clay said. "Nothing else we can do. Getting scared won't help. Try to think about something else."

I haven't named this horse yet, he thought. Russell said he'd never named him either, that I could give him whatever name I wanted. "Starbuck," Clay said aloud. "After the little town where my mother and my uncle grew up. Steer us out of here, Starbuck. Take us up high where you came from, to the Escalante Mountains. But hurry if you please."

The drops began to fall. They splashed sporadically in the shallow river with unlikely force, as if stones were being cast into the water. Several hit Clay's hat, and one his face. That was a raindrop? It seemed about like a liquid baseball!

Lightning tore down between the walls with a whine like an incoming artillery shell in a war movie and he heard a *Craack!* that sounded like it should have been produced by the canyon wall itself splitting open. This is no movie, he told himself. This is not a movie.

Curly was running around under Starbuck's feet, splashing in the shallow stream. The thunder must have rumbled him right off his perch. Clay dismounted and swept Curly up, got back on the horse with Curly in his lap.

There was the narrow opening of the third canyon, up ahead on the left. He knew it would lead him up onto the top. But how quickly? Should I take it or should I stay with the Escalante?

As yet the storm hadn't broken. Keep scouring the sides of the Escalante for places to get up. Where? Where?

Now he stood at the mouth of the third canyon. It had a dirt bottom and a tiny creek flowing out of it. Box elder trees and cottonwoods. Didn't he have to try it? How many side canyons could dump into the Escalante in fifty miles? All their waters would be combined this close to the Colorado. Wouldn't he have a better chance in one smaller canyon, especially if he could go fast and get up and out? Sam Yazzie mentioned a cliff ruin up this canyon. How far? Could he climb to it? Could he reach it in time? Could the burro and the horse?

Don't think anymore. Thunder's rumbling, lightning's snapping. Go. Go as fast as you can.

The rope back to Pal tightened. Pal was planting her

feet. Now's not the time! He kicked the mustang forward and dragged the burro on.

Pal wasn't breathing right. She was wheezing and her sides were bellowing in and out. What could be wrong?

A half mile up the canyon, the sky broke loose with heavy, stabbing rain and the cliffs spouted waterfalls within a minute. The bottom of this narrow, narrow canyon was running a rich, muddy red.

Wrong choice, Clay realized. You don't leave a wider canyon for a narrower one. The water's going to come through here deep and fast real quick, and I don't have time to get back to the river, or do I?

He turned them around, and that's when he saw it through sheets of rain. The cliff dwelling hadn't been visible from downcanyon. Safe haven if he could reach it! His eyes traced a possible route up through the ledges to the delicate cluster of cliff houses nested under an arching stone roof.

He heard a roar and saw a surging wall of water coming their way. Starbuck was already climbing.

With agility to rival the burro's, the mustang scrambled and clawed his way up and out of reach of the floodwater now raging below them.

Up, up, up. At last they gained the safe, dry, chalky floor of the alcove. Trembling, Clay got off his horse and set the tiny dog down. Curly shook himself out and looked around. Clay spun as he realized Pal was lying down with her pack fully loaded. She'd hadn't done that since the second day. "What's wrong, Pal? We won't go any farther today, okay? We should be safe here."

The creek was racing, flooding, rising. Walls of red water overtook previous walls of red water. This was the sort of rain that carves these canyons, Clay realized. Higher and closer toward them the red waters rose. He pulled Pal back to her feet and unloaded her. The canyon walls reverberated with thunder and the rain slashed at the wall across from them for another half hour. It was strange to see the bright foliage of trees in the red torrent. Every few minutes entire trees would come floating by, and underneath them you could hear an ominous grinding as boulders walked their way down down to the Escalante. Even though his mind told him they were safe where they were, his heart pounded with terror and excitement.

The rain quit suddenly. Still, the waters rose until finally they crested safely below the ruin. For a thousand years this place had remained intact. A thousand years and an afternoon. Thank you, Ancient Ones.

He could breathe easily now, he could look around.

Clay crawled into the little rooms and looked out the keyhole-shaped doorways to the flooding creek. Suddenly he felt himself back in time, and a chill ran through him. Others had sheltered in this same place a thousand years before and survived floods like the one he'd just witnessed.

At the rear of the alcove he found pictures left by those long-vanished cliff dwellers painted in white pigment on the rock. Handprints, trapezoidal human figures with antennas like spacemen, animal drawings that looked like deer or maybe sheep. He found spirals chipped into the stone.

Pal was lying down again. She was breathing heavily, panting. Obviously she was sick—it must have been all that clover she ate. She'd always seemed fat, but now she looked bloated like those cows you hear about that get into feed that's too rich and then bloat up with gas until they burst and die. The only thing you could do was lance them with a knife, if you knew how, and let the gas out. But he wouldn't know where to begin!

Curly was sniffing around Pal's backside, and now Clay could see that Pal had one of those back legs up in the air and was kicking the air with it. Her sides were heaving and she was breathing harder, groaning. She was going to die in a minute! He pulled out his pocket knife—what was he going to do?

Curly seemed awful excited there, by Pal's tail, and Clay took a look.

"Holy cow," he whispered. A little burro face and two little hoofs were coming his way out Pal's backside, all wrapped up in a filmy sack, alive and wide-eyed.

16

By morning the baby burro was on its feet frisking around. He would leap suddenly into the air, then come down in a whole other direction and gallop off. Clay grabbed him to keep him from prancing over the edge. His long ears and huge head seemed all out of proportion to his body and gave him a comical appearance. Mike, have I got some news for you, Clay was telling himself. Guess what Hubcap Willie didn't tell us about Pal, maybe didn't even know. There can't be a cuter baby animal in all of creation. You should see the white rings around his eyes, his white mouth, his little hoofs.

Curly was licking the baby burro's face, freshly wet with milk.

"I just had an idea," Clay announced. "*Ito* means 'little one' in Spanish. Let's call you Burrito! Little burro!"

Below, the creek still ran red, but had subsided nearly to its normal trickle. But the going would be more difficult now. Not all of the rubble had been swept downcanyon. He wanted to find his way out of this canyon and up onto that open country above. That wasn't going to be easy, especially with the baby burro. Burrito didn't seem to be able to predict which way his legs were going to go.

The backpack! I'll bet he'd fit in the backpack!

When Clay was all set to go, he tried it. Sure enough, Burrito made a perfect fit. Clay shouldered the pack; it was quite a sensation to look out of the corner of your eye and see that face and those ears. Burrito's legs were held so snugly, he didn't even bother to kick.

Less than a mile up the canyon, where the top of a talus slope met the slickrock, Clay found a horse ladder angling up to a trail that clearly led out of the canyon. He walked his string of horse and burro up it, and within an hour he found himself on a sea of rolling white slickrock on top of the canyons.

When the footing was good, Clay could give Burrito his legs and let him frolic his way toward Escalante, nursing along the way. The first day, the baby burro tired easily, and Clay mostly carried him in the backpack. The second day Clay was able to ride his pony half the time while Burrito walked, and by the third day, when they had to be nearing Escalante at last, Burrito had complete command of his legs and had no trouble keeping up. As if for his own pride, and just to be with the little burro, Curly had taken to his feet as well.

The whole while Clay had been paralleling the road that led from Escalante down to the Hole-in-the Rock crossing, where Sam Yazzie had told about the Mormons lowering wagons down to the river a long time ago. Occasionally he could see the plumes of dust from the pickups. But he didn't want to follow a dusty road into Escalante. He wanted to come into town reading the contours of the land.

He was following a wash upstream that was leading him out of the slickrock country and into the grassy valley he had glimpsed ahead at the foot of the mountains. A couple of big-eyed yearling cows watched him go by, then clattered downstream.

Clay's spirits soared as he imagined himself meeting his

uncle after all this time. He sat up a little straighter in the saddle and tugged at his worn black hat. Funny, he'd even forgotten about it. The hat had become a part of him. Now it was ringed with the hammered nickels, the silver buffaloes. At his neck, the red coral; on his wrist, the beautiful bracelet. Riding toward Escalante on his painted pony with the many-colored saddle blanket and the silver bridle, he felt like he was riding on clouds. "*Bik'é hozhoni*," he said aloud.

After all the miles he'd come, and all the turns in all the canyons, nothing could have prepared him for the suddenness, the shock of turning a bend in the wash and meeting, right there, a girl on horseback.

Clay reined in Starbuck. Curly too stopped in his tracks, just as dumbfounded. Right in front of him, a girl on a palomino horse. Under a gray Stetson, a girl with a single long braid down her back. A girl in a western shirt and jeans with an open, pretty face and brown eyes, and a smile on that face quickly replacing her surprise.

Suddenly three black-and-white Border collies came racing down the wash from behind her, barking protectively and enthusiastically as if to make up for having been off chasing a rabbit when they should have been out in front. She called them off and they went about the business of getting acquainted with Curly, who being no fool, had quickly shown his belly in the presence of a superior force. Along Burrito's spine, the hairs were all standing straight on end.

The girl's eyes took in the painted pony underneath him, the packed burro, the baby burro, and looked back at him inquisitively.

"Where you headed?" she asked, and let her horse take a few steps closer, until there was almost no distance between them.

"Esca—" He tried to say *Escalante*, but the word tripped

120

over itself in his dry throat and fell short. "Escalante," Clay said, clearing his throat. He glimpsed her face again, those eyes, and he saw clouds and mesas, stars, the desert fresh after a rain, a girl riding a rainbow over all of it. . . . His heart was beating madly in his chest, and he knew if he tried to speak again he wouldn't be able to speak at all. He couldn't stand it. If only he'd had a little warning. Anything he was going to say would be wrong, he knew it. Alarms were sounding in his head: you're about to make a fool of yourself, you're about to make a fool of yourself, you're about to make a fool of yourself. . . .

She sensed his extreme reticence, and her eyes went back to the packed burro and the baby burro.

Clay was grasping at straws, and it suddenly occurred to him that his best chance of survival was in playing a man of few words.

"You've come a long way?" she asked.

"Yep."

"I guess you've already told me where you're heading." She seemed to be saying she knew the code, you don't ask a man of few words much when you meet him by chance on the trail.

Her dogs were looking up at her, wondering what next.

"You haven't by any chance seen some steers?" she asked him.

"Yep," he said. "Two." If he would have thought of it he could have said where, but he was responding so cautiously it was hard to get that many words out without checking each one first to see if wasn't going to turn on him.

Her eyebrows lifted under that gray Stetson. Dark eyebrows, dark crescent moons lying down. "We're missing two. I've been searching all morning—I've been searching for a couple of days."

121

Clay swallowed, and guessed he could manage a few words. "Two's what I seen."

He'd surprised himself with "I seen." He never talked like that. Now she was looking at him again. He shouldn't have said anything. He should've held up two fingers.

She seemed to be waiting for him to speak again, and so did Curly, who was looking at him oddly as well, curious perhaps about his grammar. Suddenly it hit him that she was waiting for more about the steers, and he hiked his thumb back over his shoulder. "Down this wash," he managed. "Just a few minutes ago."

Her eyes lingered. It felt like she was looking at his hatband and the Navajo bracelet on his wrist. He couldn't tell. Barely a glimpse of her and he was lost in clouds and mesas and canyons.

"Much obliged," she said, and with a hand signal to her dogs that sent them running on the scout downstream, she gave him a smile and clucked to her horse, and was passing him by.

"Same here," Clay replied, then as soon as he said it, he knew it sounded stupid. What was he obliged for? As he clucked to his own horse, he thought, I don't even cluck right. I sounded like I'm calling a chicken, and I only hope she didn't hear that. When he thought he might be safely out of sight he held up and glanced back, and sure enough she was gone. Now he knew what he was obliged for. He was obliged for the opportunity to make a fool of himself, which he'd managed despite all odds. How difficult would it have been to have a simple conversation with her?

Clay rode along not even noticing that the wash was giving way to open lands and ranch houses here and there, corrals and barns, or even that he was following a dirt road now. He could have asked her name for starters. When she asked if he'd come a long way, he could have answered "Monument Valley" and it would have been a whole lot to

122

say in just two words. Then she would have started to ask him about his trip and he could have told her some. He could have told her about Burrito being born, she would have liked that.

Then he remembered the first thing he should have asked her. He needn't have worried about talking about himself. He should have asked about his uncle. Probably she'd heard of him. She lived around here!

Where she lived, he'd never know. He didn't even know her name. Mike would have learned her name. Mike would have had a conversation with her. If Mike had seen what had just happened, Mike would have razzed him no end. Well, Mike wasn't here. Good thing.

When Escalante came into sight, his heart soared despite himself. Forget her! What about Uncle Clay? The very idea, after all the places he'd been, that Uncle Clay might be right here, right now . . . He could feel his uncle's presence.

Probably he couldn't even remember her face. No, there it was, clear as a bell. Tanned from being out in the sun, bright smile, brown eyes tinged with yellow, dark eyebrows almost black.

Forget her! Think about Uncle Clay! Well, maybe she hadn't thought he was a complete fool. What had he actually said? Very little . . . He smiled to himself, and then his smile turned into a grimace as he heard himself saying "Yep . . . Yep . . . Yep . . ."

As he entered the town through back streets, Clay had the feeling something about it was different from any town he'd seen before. What was it? It had the look of an old town, lots of old brick, two-story houses, but that wasn't it. The streets looked much wider than regular city streets. It was the width of the streets and the size of the lots. That was it, and the huge gardens and chicken coops in the back-

123

yards. You couldn't really call them yards. Each lot was more like a miniature farm. Goats here, a milk cow there, rabbits in cages, sheds everywhere with lumber and hay and coils of wire fencing and all kinds of who-knows-what. There were lots of little kids around, and some of them stopped playing to watch him and his animals go by.

When he reached the last house before the paved street that ran through town, he asked a pair of legs that were sticking out from under the front end of an old truck if he might get some directions.

A bald head streaked with engine grease swung out by a wheel, and said "Shoot."

Clay said, "I'm lookin' for a man name of Clay Jenkins. Can you tell me where he is?"

A funny expression came over the man's face, and he said, "Clay Jenkins, rodeo star?"

"That's the man."

For some reason, the man thought this was amusing. He had a stupid grin on his face as he got up from under the truck and wiped his hands on his overalls. "See that big building over yonder?"

"On the main street?"

"No, the biggest one in town, two streets back. That's where he lives." As he spoke, he looked Burrito over, and the packed burro and Curly, and he thought something was terribly amusing.

"Do you know if he's there now?"

"Yes sir, I believe he is."

"Much obliged," Clay said abruptly, and left the man standing there enjoying his chuckle.

Clay crossed the main street and followed the dirt streets on the other side toward the tall building made of large blocks of stone. He was surprised to learn that his uncle was living inside a building at all. He'd pictured him living out in a canyon nearby and cooking over a campfire. You wouldn't think he'd be rounding up wild horses from a house in town, like a boardinghouse or something.

Clay could feel the goose bumps rising on his arms, on his neck, as he approached the big building. He was surprised to find that it was a public building. In fact it was the courthouse.

He tied Starbuck and Pal to a bench in the park across the street, and then he retied his neckerchief and straightened his hat. Burrito went to nursing; he was always hungry. The man under the truck had to be wrong, but he'd go inside and find out. Someone in there would know.

Clay walked up the broad steps, Curly right beside him, and he walked inside and down the hallway. It felt strange to be walking on a floor. He asked at the first office, the county clerk's. The woman there looked at him and looked at the little dog at his feet, and said, "You better go back outside and ask at the office at the back of the building."

People sure were different in Escalante, he thought. Maybe they don't see many folks from the outside.

He led Starbuck, Pal, and Burrito around the back, and discovered it was the sheriff's office. These people really were confused. On the other hand, it made sense that the sheriff would know where everybody was. He tied his animals to another bench, on the grass to the side of the building.

Inside, Clay stood at the counter and waited a long time for someone to show up. There wasn't a bell or anything. At last a big lady walked in, kind of old but not real old, with a beehive of silver hair. She had a mop and a bucket in her hand. "Sheriff's out for the day, dispatcher's out for lunch—what can I do for you?"

He took off his hat and he picked Curly up. "I'm looking for Clay Jenkins," he said.

The old lady kind of squinted, and said a little suspiciously, "And what's your business?"

125

"I'm trying to find out where he lives. They told me to ask here."

"Well he lives here, in a manner of speaking."

"You hear that, Curly? Whereabouts, Ma'am?"

She put a few fingers to her chin. "What are you to him?"

"I'm his nephew. I'm Clay Lancaster. He's my mother's brother."

Her face lit up and all the wrinkles in her face sang a different tune. "Why didn't you say so? How far have you come to see him?"

"From Seattle, Ma'am."

"Seattle, Washington?"

"Yes, Ma'am."

"My, my . . . call me Aunt Violet, everyone else does."

She opened the swinging half door for him and gestured with her head toward a set of wide stairs leading down. She took a small ring of keys out of her dress pocket and said, "Never said anything about relatives coming to visit."

Clay followed her down the stairs. Just as soon as he turned the corner and met a fence of bars across the wide hall and could see into a basement full of cells, it occurred to him that his uncle was in jail.

17

Clay held his breath. Curly's toenails clicked on the con-
crete floor as the old lady led them past the empty cells.
All of them were empty. His heart was pounding. He didn't
know what to think. His uncle was in jail! The long walk
ended as the woman called eagerly, just before they reached
the last cell on the right, "Visitor to see you, Clay!"

The man had just risen to his feet and put down a
paperback book.

He recognized his uncle at once through the bars and
under that black hat, even though it had been a long time.
Here he was at last, the lanky man with the angular face
and dark eyes, those crow's-feet around his eyes smiling
even when he wasn't smiling. And the dark, three-day
beard. Still there, the faraway look in his eyes. But where
was his All-Around Cowboy belt buckle, the big silver belt
buckle?

His uncle was looking him up and down, looking at the
jewelry, returning to his face. Then he broke into that
beautiful smile with that chipped tooth. "If I live to be a
hundred . . ." Uncle Clay marveled. "Look who's all
grown-up."

"I'm workin' on it," Clay said with a grin.

"Well you're nearly as tall as I am."

"I grew about six inches just the last year."

"If you aren't a pair," Aunt Violet said. "Two peas in a pod."

Curly barked suddenly, wanting to be included.

"My dog, Curly," Clay announced.

"I'm going to leave you boys," the old woman said. "I've got some cooking to attend to."

"I take it you've met Aunt Violet," Uncle Clay said. "Best cook in the county, maybe the state."

"I'm going to give you boys the run of the downstairs," she said as she jingled her keys and opened the cell door. "Be back in a bit."

Uncle Clay stepped out and shook Clay's hand, firm and long. "Man is it good to see you. Where's Mike? How's your mother?"

"Mom'll be back at the end of the month—she's in Guatemala."

"You were telling me she'd gone down there for the summer. Good for her—I was real happy to hear it."

"Mike's in Seattle. When you called, we had a really bad connection. I couldn't tell anything you were saying."

"I know. But at least you heard I was in Escalante."

"I didn't even hear that! What I heard didn't make any sense to me. But what are you doing in jail here?"

"Oh, well, I shouldn't be in here for long. I got into some trouble over some horses. I should be out soon. Here, let's pull up a chair—" His uncle spun and pulled the chair out of his cell, then went for a second from another cell. Clay stared into his uncle's cell, at the toilet, the bunk, the barred window that looked up to the outside. He still couldn't believe his uncle was in jail.

"I like the hat," his uncle said with a grin. "I like the Navajo jewelry. So tell me, you've got me stumped. How in the world did you find me?"

128

"That's a long story. . . ." Clay said. "Take a look out one of those windows on this side. I've got three friends out there, and you might recognize one of them."

His uncle stepped onto a bunk in one of the open cells. "Three friends . . . now who could that be . . ." He looked out, then looked again. "Lord, Lord." His uncle's voice was suddenly overcome with emotion. "Yes, I know that horse. It's one of the first two."

Stepping down from the bunk, his uncle said, "Sam Yazzie's who made your bracelet!"

Clay nodded. "I've come a long way," he said quietly. "I started out in Monument Valley—I came across Russell's grandparents there."

Tears were gathering in his uncle's eyes. "To find me? You came all this way to find me?"

Clay shrugged. "It's so different from back home out here . . . I really like it, and I thought it would be an adventure. I thought it was the kind of thing . . . that you would do."

His uncle took his handkerchief out of his pocket and wiped his eyes, then blew his nose once, twice.

Uncle Clay was laughing through his tears. "Look at me. Bawling like a baby and honking like a goose. And here I thought I was pretty much alone in the world."

"I know about what happened. That you were married, that you lost your wife."

The man looked up, and then away. Clay had never seen desolation in his uncle's eyes before. "It was hard, Clay, so hard I thought I'd just die from the grief. I've been alone my whole life, until Lily. When I met her, I could see the rest of my life in front of me. I loved her. . . . I'm awful sorry I didn't write, Clay. I've been trying to work up to it, and that's why I called finally."

"I'm just sorry about what happened. I'm really sorry, Uncle Clay."

129

"They say 'don't look back,' but I'll remember those days with her and her family as long as I draw breath. They were the best of my life. It pleases me so much, that you've just come from the Yazzies. You and I've got a lot to catch up on."

"We waited at the Colorado on the twenty-seventh for you to bring the horses down. What happened?"

His uncle flashed that broken-tooth smile. "Got caught!" Then he winked and said, "I know Aunt Violet's uncommon nice, but this isn't a hotel she's running, you know."

"What happened to the horses?"

"It's a real shame—that bunch is off to the slaughterhouse, and now the same thing will happen to the last band up there."

"There's still some up there then?"

His uncle's face lit up. "A buckskin stallion with a black stripe down his back and rings on his lower legs, a lead mare as blue as a mountain bluebird, and about a dozen other mares, mostly with colts. They're the last ones. After that last bunch I was going to head for Seattle and look you and Mike and your mother up. Do some fishing with you, maybe even go back to working on the salmon boats."

"How soon can you get out?"

"Soon I think. A lot of people around here don't think all that highly of Barlow and what he's doing."

I've heard that name, Clay thought. Yes, from Sam Yazzie. "Isn't he the one that's selling the wild horses? The one that wouldn't take your wife to the doctor?"

"The same. But let's not talk about him. I want to hear all about your journey with Curly here and those long-eared rascals outside. Don't you just love 'em?"

Aunt Violet was wheeling in a cart. She sang out, "You boys hungry for fried chicken?"

"This fellow's come all the way from Monument

Valley, Aunt Violet. Bound to be hungry. He's a regular vagabond."

"And they say they don't make 'em like they used to. I've been thinking, it's such a nice day, why don't you boys take your trays outside—you could see your nephew's animals up close, Clay."

"I don't see why not," his uncle said with a wink. "We'll be good."

"I know you will. Sheriff Darling won't mind. Behind the building you won't raise much notice. No one'll mind."

"C'mon, Curly," his uncle said. "We're moving it outdoors. I've got a lot of catching up to do with your buddy here."

"What did they do with your horse? Was it one of the wild horses once?"

"No, me and Loosa have been together a good while. She's in the sheriff's corral in the next block over here. She's fine, they're taking good care of her."

"That reminds me—where's your All-Around Cowboy buckle? You always wore that buckle."

His uncle shrugged and said quietly, "I . . . I left it behind."

Clay bought a few groceries at the general store in Escalante and then he headed out of town to find himself a place to camp. He felt drawn by the cliffs above a valley a few miles beyond town, and he steered that way. It looked inviting when he reached it: good grass and tall pines and a clear stream that ran steady if only a few inches deep. Above the valley, sheer red walls towered on both sides with fir trees clinging to the high ledges.

A road led up the valley, probably a logging road leading into the mountains. But he preferred to stick to the creek bottom.

The spot didn't look different to him than any other

131

spot on the sandy creekbed. Shallow water was rippling its way downstream in undulating waves over miniature sand hills. Not enough water to concern a burro.

He wasn't watching that closely. He was walking in front of Starbuck, leading him because the pony had started to favor his left front leg as they left Escalante. There might have been something to see at that spot in the creekbed but he wasn't looking all that closely. He was on the deck of a salmon boat with his uncle, and they were catching salmon until their arms were about to fall off. They were heading up the Inside Passage toward Ketchikan, Alaska, with the steep, dark mountains wrapped in mist rising straight out of the sea. He'd always liked that name, Ketchikan, and thought he might get there one day. . . .

Suddenly Clay was chest-deep in the creekbed. Quicksand! He tried to kick his way out, but succeeded only in kicking his way out of his cowboy boots and worsening his predicament. Now only his head and shoulders were free. He thought he'd better quit struggling and breathe easy with his arms out as wide as he could keep them, and see if it would give him time to think.

Curly stood wisely back from the soft spot and eyed him one way, then the other, finding it unusual that his companion had only a head and arms and a hat.

"Throw me a rope, Curly," Clay joked desperately, trying as fast as he could to think of only one of the dozens of ways he'd seen dogs rescue kids in quicksand in shows like "Lassie" and "Rin Tin Tin." He couldn't think of even one. Apparently Curly couldn't either.

Curly reacted by barking in his high-pitched voice while Pal and Starbuck waited patiently for him to extricate himself. It crossed Clay's mind, even at a time he couldn't afford distractions, that Pal had been right about not trusting water. Her big eyes, ringed with white, seemed to be saying, "You didn't listen" as she nudged Burrito away from the danger.

At least he wasn't sinking any further. Curly continued to bark, and the minutes went by. Days it seemed like. The quicksand had him locked up but good. At least it's cool, he thought. What a way to beat the heat. If I'd thought to wear a whistle around my neck, I'd sure blow on it about now.

Then he heard barking, not Curly's but deeper barks from bigger dogs, and suddenly those black-and-white dogs he'd met earlier in the day showed up, those Border collies. One of them started toward him to investigate, but stopped and lifted one paw in the air, then wheeled around and returned to the bank. In a minute Clay was looking at the girl riding up, the dark-haired girl of the clouds and mesas and rainbows, the girl with the gray Stetson and the long braid down her back, the one who had taken his breath away. Somewhere close by, those two steers were complaining to the afternoon.

"We meet again," she said with a smile. All he could think of was to be polite, and so he lifted his hat from his head, and greeted her with a gentlemanly nod.

18

"Stay still," she said.

"Okay," he replied. "I won't go anywhere."

The girl with the long braid smiled as she reached for her lariat, and she dismounted in a smooth motion. Whirling the lasso around her head, she took a few steps closer. He looked up into her face, all concentration. She wasn't laughing at him, at least.

This isn't the way it's supposed to be, Clay thought. I should be saving *her*.

One thing he was glad of: his brother wasn't here to see this.

She roped him on her first try. As she mounted her horse she said, "We're going to pull you downstream so you can come out on your back with your face up. Try to backstroke if you can help us. Just like you're swimming."

Her palomino horse responded as if he were trained for the occasion. It all worked like she said. He flopped around like a fish, but at last he found himself on solid ground. Clay picked himself up, freed himself from the rope, and said quietly, "Thanks. Thanks for pulling me out."

"It wasn't anything," she said with a shy smile. "Roping a calf is a lot harder."

There he was, standing in front of her in his bare feet. He couldn't have looked more ridiculous. He knew he'd never see those expensive cowboy boots again.

"I like the baby burro, and its mother, and your little dog."

"Thanks," Clay said dispiritedly. It had taken a lot out of him, making a fool of himself twice in one day with the same girl.

"And your horse—I think that's the most beautiful horse I've seen in my life."

"Thanks. Something's wrong with his foot, the front left one."

"Really? I'll take a look."

Clay went to unrigging Pal's diamond hitch to get at his hiking boots.

"You sure surprised me this morning," she said, as she took her time to get acquainted with his horse. "Where in the world did you come from? I've never seen you around here before."

"Monument Valley." He felt a small surge of pride saying it. Maybe he could talk to her, even if he had made a fool of himself—twice. Maybe that would even help. He'd gotten it over with.

"Really? No kidding—you came from Monument Valley? I've always wanted to go there."

"That's where I started," he said, taking his first deep breath since the creekbed had squeezed the starch out of him.

"You out here on your own?"

"Pretty much."

"That's amazing. Here's the problem, he had a big pebble in his frog."

"Frog?"

"The soft spot in the center of his hoof. Funny name, eh?"

135

Clay laughed. This girl made you feel good. It was easy to be with her, even if she was so pretty.

"I like your bracelet, and your hatband."

"Thanks." He was lacing up his boots. "I've seen a lot of places since I started out, but this valley's special. It's got the red cliffs and the big trees at the same time."

She seemed so pleased. "Really?"

"Sure."

"I live here—just a couple miles up. My family's is the only place in the valley."

With an occasional hand signal and not a word spoken, she sent the dogs to outflank the steers whenever they strayed. As they rode up the valley side by side, they were looking for a good place for him to camp. But they got so busy talking they weren't looking for campsites anymore. Her name was Sarah and it was the easiest thing in the world to talk with her. It didn't matter that he loved her—and that it was hopeless. He could set that aside. He could talk to her about the country he had seen. She had that look in her eyes. She loved the wild places the way he did.

Clay tried not to talk too much, to make big of himself. He didn't want to hear himself talking that way. He wanted to set himself aside and tell her what it was like, just being out there.

But she wanted to know more and more and more. By the time they reached the end of the valley, he'd told her all about his search for Uncle Clay. He'd even told her that the horse he was riding was born in the Escalante Mountains, that his uncle was in the Escalante jail.

"Clay Jenkins, the rodeo star!"

"That's him."

"Lots of people think he's right to try to save those horses—I sure do! So he's your uncle."

When Clay saw the ranch nestled in that green valley

136

under those red walls, with its fenced pastures, orchard, barn, and the creek running right by a two-story log house, he said, "Sarah, you live in heaven."

"My dad built our house," she said fondly. "He brought the logs out of the mountains. That's him coming this way."

Her father came riding up on a sorrel horse, his eyes asking unspoken questions about what his daughter had dragged home, this muddy fellow with the unusual entourage. "Sarah, you found those steers!"

"Dad, this is Clay Lancaster. He's from Seattle, and he walked and rode all the way from Monument Valley. He came to find his uncle, who's Clay Jenkins."

The smile playing in the tall man's eyes spread to the rest of his face. He said, "Well, I'll be."

"I think he could use a place to stay for a little while."

"He's got it," her father said, reaching over to shake Clay's hand. "Bud Darling."

"I'm glad to meet you, Mr. Darling."

"Please," he said with a laugh that his daughter echoed, "anything but that. If you had my name, you'd much prefer people just left it at 'Bud.' "

"Thanks for the hospitality, Bud." Still, Clay thought, it doesn't feel right to call him by his first name.

"My wife likes 'Mrs. Darling' just fine. Somehow it suits her better than me. Yours must be quite a story and she'll want to hear it. Libby and Nora will too, and I haven't even heard it yet myself. You're quite welcome here, Clay. You take care of him Sarah, I'll look after these steers."

As they rode in, two girls flew out of the house onto the porch all excited and big-eyed at the sight of Clay, the packed burro with the little dog nestled on top, and especially the baby burro frisking alongside. Unlike their sister Sarah in jeans, both of these girls wore long dresses. Like homemade, Clay thought. The older of the two had a long ponytail that swung from side to side as she ran.

137

"Libby's ten and Nora's five," Sarah said.

Mrs. Darling, also in a long dress, appeared right behind them as Nora made a beeline for Burrito and hugged him around the neck. The little girl in pigtails looked up at Clay and said, "This boy sure is muddy."

"Where'd you find him, Sarah?" asked her sister Libby.

"She fished me out of the creek," Clay explained.

Sarah laughed. "Biggest fish I ever caught."

As Clay soaked in the tub, he could see Mrs. Darling down by the creek rinsing the mud off his jeans and his shirt. He'd tried to save that chore for himself and thought he'd won, but there she was. She had all of his clothes, and she'd slipped him some of Mr. Darling's through the bathroom door. It was embarrassing. He hadn't exactly been looking after clothes washing on his travels. Now and again he'd rinsed his clothes and lay them out on the rocks to dry, but he'd never picked up any laundry soap and he hadn't thought to use his bar soap on his clothes.

Libby and Nora were playing outside. Nora was shrieking with joy and Libby was yelling "Look at him go! Look at him go!"

The little spot in the window he could see through showed Burrito galloping across the yard with Curly in ear-flapping pursuit. The little burro suddenly snorted and leaped into the air, pirouetted, and raced off around the house.

For the first time, Clay tried out her first name with her last. Sarah Darling. Sarah Darling. Sarah Darling. Her name shook him up so badly when he heard himself repeating it, he thought he'd better not think about it for a while.

Suppertime. He felt so grateful and so . . . clean. He'd scrubbed himself raw to try to present himself suitably.

Sarah's father was saying the grace, and he was having a lot to say. Dark-haired like Sarah, he had a bit of gray showing in his sideburns. The roast beef was steaming on the platter and it sure looked good. They'd raised everything on the table themselves: the beef, the potatoes, the carrots, the salad greens. He felt a little funny in her father's clothes. The shirt felt like it was starched. He sneaked a glimpse of Sarah. She'd changed from her jeans into a long homemade dress like her mother's and her sisters'. Sarah Darling, Sarah Darling, Sarah Darling . . . Libby was watching him take that glance at Sarah, and then she was watching her big sister. Libby had a curious little smile on her face. "Amen," Mr. Darling concluded, and Clay whispered "Amen" along with the rest of the family.

"Did you get through to your brother Mike?" Mrs. Darling asked as she passed him the gravy.

"Yes, Ma'am, he was pretty excited about me finding Uncle Clay. Awful surprised to find out he was in jail. And he read me a letter from my mother. It's the first one that's gotten through since she was actually in Guatemala."

"And how's she doing?"

"Perfect. The people are really poor I guess, but really nice. She likes being down there as much as she thought she would."

"It's quite brave," Mrs. Darling commented, though she looked a little skeptical. "Did you and Mike talk about how you'll get home?"

"Yes, Ma'am—with Uncle Clay on the train, closest we can catch one."

Libby said wistfully, "I'd like to ride on a train one day."

"Come out and see us sometime!" Clay proposed. "You could stay with us while you're there. Uncle Clay and I are going to go out on a salmon boat. He might take up fishing for a living. Do you like fishing, Mr.—Bud?"

"Mr. Bud!" little Nora giggled.

At the mention of fishing, a profound look of happiness had come over Mr. Darling's face.

"Does he ever," Mrs. Darling explained. "Sarah too."

"Fishing for a living . . ." Mr. Darling rhapsodized. His deep green eyes reminded Clay of the depths of his favorite mountain lake in the Cascades. "That wouldn't bother me one bit."

"It's different out there," Clay said. "I hope you'll like it. It's pretty and everything, but where we live, it's not like this. We live on a regular street, you know, with houses close together on both sides."

Clay could see Sarah and her sisters trying to imagine it.

"Like in town in Escalante?" Libby suggested.

"Oh, they're a lot closer than that. Uncle Clay probably wouldn't live with us or anything—he'd feel too cooped up. He'll probably live in one of the little fishing towns. Or maybe he'll live on a boat."

"Your uncle is much admired around here, by some, that is," Mrs. Darling observed. "Some people even think of him as a sort of Robin Hood for the wild horses. I know Sarah does."

A serious expression came over Mr. Darling's face. "It's really pretty extraordinary, Clay, what's happened here since your uncle came along. People are starting to wonder if it's right, what's happening to these horses. You see, this is cattle country, and it's hard enough making a living around here as it is. Most of the cattle grazing is on government land that the ranchers lease. It's true that the wild horses forage for the same graze that we need for our cattle. Except for the mountains, people call this land around here 'ten-thirty country.' You explain it, Sarah," he asked with a wink in her direction.

140

"Sarah's as good a cowboy as Daddy," volunteered little Nora, eager to get in on the conversation.

Sarah blushed. " 'Ten-thirty country' means your cow has to have a mouth ten feet across, and has to be able to run thirty miles an hour to find enough grass around here to stay alive. You've seen the country around here, Clay, not much for a cow or a horse to eat."

"The country won't be so big or beautiful without the wild horses," Mr. Darling said. "But there's nothing to protect them—in fact, the law's all on the other side. Barlow has a legal contract with the government to take out every last one, and people here do believe in obeying the law."

"The horses should come before a piece of paper," Sarah said with emotion. "No one asked the horses."

Nora whispered, "They're making them into *chicken food.*"

"We hope they won't deal with your uncle too severely," Mrs. Darling said. "We hope he can just get on that train with you, wherever you're going to catch it, and that'll be the end of it. It's not like he hurt anybody."

Libby said importantly, "Daddy's brother's the sheriff."

Clay's eyes found Mr. Darling's. "How soon does he think Uncle Clay will get out?"

"The sheriff is hoping your uncle will be able to pay a fine and agree not to come back around here again."

"Let's not talk about that anymore," said Mrs. Darling. "Let's have some peach pie and ice cream and think about what you kids are going to do tomorrow."

"There's a John Wayne movie that just came to town," Libby said.

Clay almost jumped. "What is it? I like John Wayne movies."

Libby ran into the living room for the newspaper. "*The Man Who Shot Liberty Valance,*" she called.

"That's the one I've been looking for!" Clay declared. "I'd give anything to see that movie."

Mr. Darling laughed. "Fifty cents ought to do it. Sarah likes John Wayne too. Sarah, your mother and I were going into town tomorrow night anyway, to meet with the other people planning the county fair—why don't we drop the four of you off at the movies on the way?"

Clay and Sarah nodded in agreement.

"Let's get these dishes done," Mrs. Darling said. "It's getting late, and we've all had a big day, especially Clay here."

Everyone got up from the table. Clay helped Sarah with the dishes. Her sisters went off giggling to their room upstairs. Sarah's mother was finding some bedding for Clay to take out to the bunkhouse.

Sarah disappeared as he was drying the last few pans. When she came back a few minutes later she said, "I've been talking to my father. If you and I got up really early tomorrow morning, I could take you fishing up at Cyclone Lake—we could ride our horses. We'd still be back in time for the movie. Do you think you'd like that?"

19

They climbed all morning into the big pines and firs, until it started to feel almost like the Northwest, Clay thought. Starbuck seemed to be enjoying the work more than in the lower country, and as the air cooled and thinned and they entered groves of aspen and spruce, the formerly wild horse became more animated than Clay had ever seen him. "Look at him, Sarah, he's acting like a colt."

"He's back in his summer range."

"How high is Cyclone Lake?"

"It's over ten thousand feet. I'm glad we brought the dogs with us—they're having a great time. And look at Curly! Look at those little feet go! He isn't having any trouble keeping up with my dogs."

They paused on an outcrop that gave them a view of the lower country below them: the town of Escalante at the foot of the mountains, marked by the smoking tepee burner at the sawmill, and beyond the town, a world of slickrock and canyons as far as the eye could see.

"That long, narrow canyon between us and the Colorado River," Sarah said pointing, "that's Escalante Canyon, where your uncle ran the horses down. It was such a beautiful idea. It's so narrow the horses had nowhere to go but straight ahead. It's so great to think one man was able to do that by himself."

"The side canyon I climbed out of? What's it called?"

"I'm sure it was Davis Canyon. Third one up from the river, and it has a horse ladder."

"You know all this country."

"Look how much there is! Some of those canyons are so narrow you can touch both walls with your hands, and they're hundreds and hundreds of feet deep. There are so many out there, probably no one's seen them all. Sometimes the cows get down in those canyons and it takes a lot of searching to find them out."

I'd help you search for those cows, Clay thought. I wouldn't care if we never found them.

"Between us and the beginning of Escalante Canyon there's a box canyon called Death Hollow. That's where your uncle had the horses stashed before he started them down the Escalante."

"Look, Sarah—there's Navajo Mountain, all by itself over there across the Colorado. I was right up close to it."

They spread out a checkered tablecloth on the grassy bank of Cyclone Lake, and brought out their sandwiches. Nothing could be more perfect than this green grass and the music of her voice, watching the clouds go by and sharing a picnic lunch. There could never be another day like this one. There could never be another girl like this one.

Curly showed up and licked him on the face. He wished it were so easy to kiss Sarah, just like that. Well, not just *like* that.

Clay looked at her long, and she looked back at him, and his heart was beating like thunder. He felt like he was about to kiss her, but it felt like being about to step over a cliff. It was the scariest moment he'd faced in his life.

"The dogs," Sarah said suddenly. Her dogs were standing frozen like Border collie statues, and even Curly was standing still like a statue.

Clay looked in the direction the dogs were looking. Way down near the end of the lake and on the other side, horses were coming down to the water.

"Wild horses," Sarah whispered. "Keep low!"

The dogs knew not to bark. Even Curly kept quiet.

"Look," Sarah whispered. "That's the lead mare bringing them down to the lake. She looks blue even from here."

" 'Blue as a mountain bluebird,' " Clay said thoughtfully. "Sarah, these must be the ones Uncle Clay had his eye on. This must be that last band he told me about. The stallion's a buckskin with . . . lemme think . . . a black stripe down his back and rings on his legs. A dozen or so mares with their colts, he said."

"That's about what I count. Look, there's the stallion standing guard. With markings like those, he'd be a real throwback. You know, there's only about twenty thousand mustangs left in the whole country. The lead mare's drinking now, then the next in rank and so on. If the stallion tries to drink before all the rest are finished, the mares will run him off. I saw it once."

"I count eighteen."

"They'll be dead soon, and Barlow will make his five cents a pound. Aren't they beautiful? They probably are the last ones. Let's see how close we can get to them, Clay."

Silently they crept back into the trees, where they had left their horses, and circled the lake in the spruce. The dogs understood the need for stealth. Though Curly didn't understand Sarah's hand signals, he was taking his cues from the other dogs and he was learning fast.

Clay watched her give the hand signals too, watched how quietly her palomino moved in the woods, careful not to break a stick.

At the edge of the woods, Sarah let Clay draw alongside, and they watched the wild horses at lakeside through an opening in the woods. The stallion was drinking now. Most of the mares and colts were rolling in the mud at the edge of the lake.

"Look at that," Clay whispered.

"To protect themselves from the flies. The mud dries and gives them a thicker skin."

Suddenly a new horse galloped up, all black with a white blaze on his forehead and white stockings, and before Clay could even see how he'd done it the black had cut out the two mares and their colts who weren't in the mud, and he was herding them away as fast as he could.

The big buckskin took off in hot pursuit, and before the black could herd his prizes into the woods, the buckskin cut him off and the two stood in full display, their necks arched and their front legs pawing the ground and then pawing the air.

"I've always wanted to see this," Sarah whispered.

Clay strained to get a better look, expecting to see a big battle. Yet with no blood drawn, it wasn't but half a minute until the buckskin was racing back to the rest behind the four that had been kidnapped, nipping the trailing colt to make him go faster. "What happened?" Clay asked. "I didn't even see what happened."

"The black's probably a much younger stallion," Sarah explained. "He knew he wasn't the buckskin's match yet, so he backed down. You know what I'm thinking, Clay. . . ."

She had the most wonderful grin on her face.

"If we could possibly do it, we could hide them away and no one would ever suspect that they've been stashed away because your uncle is in jail! And then, as soon as he gets out, he can run them down the Escalante! They'd be across the Colorado and so would he, before anyone could say Jack Robinson!"

Clay's mouth dropped. "Could we do it?"

For no apparent reason, a couple of the mares nickered, and there was a distinct note of alarm in their voices.

"Maybe they smell us," Sarah whispered. "We have to make our move fast. Follow me, and hang on to your hat!"

With that she exploded out of the woods, giving signals to the dogs, and the wild horses exploded into flight as well.

"Death Hollow!" Sarah shouted.

With a grin spreading across his own face, Clay galloped to catch up as she raced to keep the stampeding horses between her and the lake. What a sight Sarah was! The mustangs tried to make a break out and toward the woods. They ran at full speed with their manes and tails flying, but her dogs headed them around the end of the lake and down into the beginning of a draw that fed off the mountain.

And then it was all pleasure, just trying to keep up with Sarah, with his heart in his throat and his legs slapping Starbuck's side and his eyes on that long dark braid that seemed to have a life of its own. Down the mountain he flew through the tall spruce and into the aspen breaks and down into the pines, enjoying an occasional glimpse over his shoulder of a small blur of white and hearing Curly's high-pitched battle cry.

It was all pleasure except for one thing. He was having the hardest time trying to keep the blocky toes of those hiking books in the stirrups. If I live through this, Clay thought, I'll get me a new pair of cowboy boots in the morning!

Rock formations started to show up, then cliffs and domes and spires of rock with the tall trees growing in niches, and the chase was dropping through sandstone formations now and into the beginnings of a canyon.

He caught up with Sarah, who'd slowed to a walk. At last they could hold up and rest. The wild horses couldn't get up the sides of the canyon unless they could fly.

"Is this it?" Clay asked, all winded. "Death Hollow?" Now Curly caught up, panting and proud.

"Not yet," she replied. "They could work their way back up to the lake from here. I know a way into Death Hollow a few miles down. That's where we'll take them."

And that's what Sarah did. She knew a place where only two horses at a time could squeeze between the rocks, and she and her dogs funneled them through the crack, all eighteen of them, and into Death Hollow. Clay helped her drag logs and brush until they'd plugged the gap behind them.

Through a world of bizarre rock formations they rode into the afternoon. They drove the horses into the bottom of Death Hollow where sufficient grass and a flowing creek would provide a sanctuary. Sarah flanked them, pushing them back upstream a ways, and then she said, "Let's go fix the fence."

Clay took a last glimpse at the horses and started down the canyon. They soon came upon an old homestead by the creek, long abandoned. Where the canyon walls narrowed to a gap a half-mile farther, they stopped to repair the high pole fence that was down in two places. "Your uncle sure put a lot of work into this," Sarah said as they lifted the first pole into position.

It didn't take long to put the fence back to rights. "Those horses aren't getting out this way," Clay commented as they stood back to admire the fence, intact once again. He lifted his hat and wiped his shirtsleeve across his forehead. "They'll be waiting right here for Uncle Clay. On to *The Man Who Shot Liberty Valance!*"

As they rode into the ranch, they felt like they were still ten thousand feet up. It was a good feeling, exchanging glances as they approached the house, having a secret between them.

Her mother was working at the sink. She was wearing rubber gloves and lifting jars of bright red tomatoes out of a steaming enamel pot. The radio was on; she'd been listening as she worked. Her apron showed she'd been through something. "How was it?" she asked Sarah brightly. Suddenly aware of his hat, Clay doffed it and held it by his side. "How was the fishing?" her mother asked.

"We forgot all about it!" Sarah replied.

Clay added, "It sure is beautiful up there, Mrs. Darling."

"I'm glad you liked it, Clay. It doesn't seem like the fishing's ever that good late in the summer anyway. Sarah, I haven't heard a peep out of Libby and Nora, and you know that's not a good sign. Would you check on them? We have to keep moving if we're going to get you to the movies on time. Your dad's got the charcoal going. We're just going to have some hamburgers and potato salad. They were up in their room getting ready for the fair."

"County fair starts this weekend," Sarah explained. "It starts the day after tomorrow, actually tomorrow night with the dance out at Dance Hall Rock."

"We hope you'll be staying through the fair, Clay. Have you ever been to a county fair?"

"No, Ma'am, but I'd sure like to. I guess they have them out there. But not where we live. I'm pretty much of a city kid, I guess. Well, not really a city kid—I guess I'm a kid from the suburbs."

"After the summer you've had I'd say you'd pass for a cowboy."

Clay smiled. "I feel like I'm from out here. They say in the Northwest, you can tell the natives because they have moss growing on their north side, but I feel like all mine must've burned off by now."

He followed Sarah into the living room. They heard something, and then they listened again. They glanced at

149

each other. Could it be? Yes it was. The unmistakable sound of small hoofs galloping.

"Uh-oh," Sarah said, and went flying upstairs.

She disappeared. Still more galloping.

Clay hesitated, then climbed the stairs. He'd better catch that rascal before he broke something of the Darlings'.

At the top of the landing he saw Burrito streak from one room into another with the girls on his heels. What in the world? Did he see what he thought he'd seen?

Clay poked his head in the doorway.

Yes indeed. Burrito was dressed to kill in a blue vest and matching blue bonnet that fit down over his ears. The baby burro was standing in the middle of a large bed, on a fancy lace bedspread, snorting loudly and all cocked for mischief. With a glance Clay realized this was the parents' bedroom. Porcelain knickknacks on low nightstands were poised delicately just waiting to crash.

"You guys . . ." Sarah was saying ominously. She was on one side of the bed, her sisters on the other.

"We've got him surrounded," Libby said.

That's when Burrito bolted, and Clay tried to grab for him. The burro galloped as if to one side, then swerved and shot right between his legs.

"Get him!" the girls were yelling, and little Nora was shrieking for joy as she and her flying pigtails chased the burro down the hallway.

"What's going on up there?" their mother was calling. "You girls should be getting ready for supper and the movies."

"Nothing, Mom," Libby called back. "We're getting ready."

Past a brightly colored room with two beds, Burrito raced into the one at the end of the hall. When they caught up with him Burrito was standing in a white wicker rocking chair and bracing himself against its motion. His ears swiveled around one at a time and pointed at them, and he snorted explosively.

"I've heard of a rocking horse before," Libby said, "but never a rocking burro."

"And look what he's standing on," Sarah said less than enthusiastically.

Nora put her little hand over her mouth. "Your dress, Sarah! Your dress for the dance!"

"I'll get him," Libby said confidently, edging closer.

And she did. When Burrito leaped from the rocker, Libby caught him in midair. Suddenly the burro was still, but he was breathing heavily. "You little devil," Libby said affectionately, and kissed him on the nose.

Sarah was arranging her dress over the top of the rocker. It was a beautiful rose color, with a neckline of embroidered flowers and the bottom circled with layers of pink and white ruffles.

"Sarah made it herself," Nora explained importantly. "Especially for the dance. This is Sarah's room."

Clay could already tell that. There was one entire shelf dedicated to figurines of horses. There must have been two dozen of them.

"Burrito's outfit is awful cute," Sarah said, and her sisters beamed. Clay scratched the inside of one of the burro's ears and explained to Libby, "He likes that."

"We're entering him in the county fair!" exclaimed Nora. "In the pets division!"

"If he wins a blue ribbon, it won't be for Best Behaved," Sarah replied.

Her sisters left to see if it might still be possible to sneak Burrito out of the house. Clay was looking around the room.

"It's a mess," Sarah said, blushing.

"No, it's not, it's just the opposite. You should see my room if you want to see a mess. I like your dress. You really made it all by yourself?"

151

"Sure."

It seemed amazing to be in her room. Right where she lives. In the heart of where she lives. His eyes were drawn to a bulletin board about half covered with blue ribbons, and under it photos of her at all different ages with ponies and big horses too. "You won all these ribbons?" he said, as he looked closely at her as a little girl.

"Don't look at those," she said. "I look terrible."

"You look . . . wonderful."

Beside the first, a second bulletin board was covered with photos clipped from movie magazines, of different movie stars and one of Monument Valley!

She wasn't speaking, she seemed bashful and uncertain. Clay's eyes were drawn back to the figurines of horses, some crystal, some porcelain, some wood. "They're beautiful," he said.

The shelf above was full of books. "*Misty of Chincoteague*," he said aloud. "Hey, I remember that book. It's about wild horses! How the Spanish conquistadores first brought them over, and they got away and went wild!"

Clay scanned the titles. "All these books are about horses!" It came to him, something he could do for her when he got back home. He had a wood-carving set he'd gotten for Christmas and never used once. If he could learn to carve well enough to send her a carving that he had made with his own hands, she would keep the horse he'd made right here along with the others.

20

Clay and Sarah were whispering when the lights went down, the big screen lit up, and the music began. They whispered through the opening credits when those words appeared across the screen, *The Man Who Shot Liberty Valance*. "Who do you think shot him?" Clay whispered. "Jimmy Stewart or John Wayne?"

"Shhhhh!" came Libby's voice amid her giggles, from right behind them. Little Nora chimed in, "They're on a date! They're on a date!"

Clay glanced from the screen, where Jimmy Stewart was stepping off the train, to Sarah's face. Her eyebrows were saying, "My sisters are pests, but there's nothing we can do about it."

He didn't mind. He'd enjoyed treating them to popcorn and soda. He was thinking of them more as pets than pests.

Back to the screen. He didn't want to miss a bit of it. What matter that her sisters were giggling behind them? It was dark, it was a movie house, and here was John Wayne bigger than life. This really was all happening to him, all in the town of Escalante, Utah, on a day he'd run wild horses out of the mountains with the girl sitting right beside him, a girl made of the stuff of his own heart.

Liberty Valance swaggered onto the screen, leering and vile, and his whip hand knocked Jimmy Stewart to the ground. "He's awful," Sarah whispered. "He's scum," Clay whispered back.

"Is he going to kiss her?" Nora asked Libby. Then the two were giggling again.

Clay pretended he didn't hear that. The movie heated up. The girls were all caught up in it now too.

When the big moment in the movie came and Clay realized the sacrifice John Wayne was making, that he would give up the girl he loved to Jimmy Stewart, that he would let her and everyone believe that it was the tenderfoot with the law books who had shot Liberty Valance, Clay couldn't keep the tears from his eyes and his hand from reaching for Sarah's. The girls were too absorbed to notice and he watched the last minutes of the movie with her hand in his. He felt her gentle grip as the joy and the sadness of the day and the movie ran back and forth between them.

The music swelled and the lights went up, and Clay was blinking away the tears. John Wayne had lived out his life and gone to his grave lonely. Clay felt sure there was nothing as miraculous in life as love. "Great movie," he said.

Sarah squeezed his hand and then their hands parted. Sarah's eyes were misty too. The girls were giggling again. People were standing up and stretching, and moving up the aisles.

"That's him," Sarah said suddenly. "Staring at us. That's Barlow, in the vest."

Clay saw the man there, across the aisle and down to the right, still seated and staring at him. Yes, at him.

Why?

Now the big man raised himself slowly, fitted his hat to his head, staring all the while. Clay could feel the fear

154

coming from the little girls—the man sent a chill through him too.

Barlow lumbered up the aisle, but as he reached their row, he stopped. They were only a few seats in and Barlow was leaning toward them. His face was hard like an anvil, and his eyes squinted with hatred.

"So you're the kid," Barlow said hoarsely. "I heard you were staying with the Darlings."

His voice made everything sound like swearing.

"So you're the big ex-rodeo star's nephew."

"That's right," Clay managed. It felt like there was no air in his lungs to talk with. I'm not going to let him bully me, he thought. "—And proud of it," he added in a louder voice.

Libby and Nora were frozen to their seats. Sarah was tensed and waiting.

The man brought his face closer, and his voice began to rasp even before he spoke. "I bet you think this is all a game, don't you kid? Your uncle stealing my horses, resting up a few days in jail. Just like in the movies, right? We'll see what you think in a few days."

Now Barlow stared at Sarah as well, and then back at Clay. "I'm not surprised you're staying with the Darlings. Well, her father and his brother Sheriff Darling are going to find that things aren't going to turn out quite the way they thought. I'm putting a stop to all this, once and for all."

With that he was gone. The big man strode up the aisle and disappeared.

"Isn't he awful," Libby said. "He thinks he's so big."

"He was worse than Liberty Valance," Nora declared.

Clay looked around. Barlow was gone. Everyone had left the theater but them.

Sarah hadn't spoken but now she did. "Horsekiller," she said between her teeth.

"I wonder what John Wayne would do to him," Libby said. "He'd take care of him."

Clay looked at Sarah. She was just as shaken as he was. "Sarah, what did he mean? What's he going to do?"

Deeply troubled, Clay said good night to the Darlings and collected Curly, then walked over to the bunkhouse in the bright moonlight. He'd sit awhile out on the porch, where he could think. What did Barlow mean? What did he know?

It wasn't but a few minutes until he saw Mr. Darling coming his way. He took a seat on the porch next to Clay.

Clay wondered if Mr. Darling had come over to talk about Barlow. Sarah had told her father all about what happened at the movies, that Barlow had made some kind of bad threat about Uncle Clay. But her father had said little about it, remaining strangely silent.

"We used to have a fair number of mountain lions around here," the rancher began slowly, as if he were talking to the night.

"Once in a while a lion would take a few calves, not many. Now the lions are about gone. We're making the world safe for cows, I guess . . . When I was a kid, younger than you are now, I saw the last wolf in these parts."

"You saw a wolf, around here?"

"Lobo Arch is named after him, down in Coyote Canyon. That wolf was likely the last survivor of a pack in the Arizona Strip, and must've swum the Colorado over to the Escalante side."

The man's voice trailed away, as he seemed to have drifted out of the present. But then he picked up his story as he reached for a pine needle on the railing that he stuck in his teeth like a straw. "That wolf had a habit of nosing through piles of tin cans and garbage out around the line shacks. Finally he put his foot in a trap hidden in one of

156

those piles. He dragged that trap ten miles before he was finally shot."

"You were there?"

"Got there right after he was killed. That wolf was the most bedraggled canine I've seen in my life. Last wolf. It was my father that shot him. And you know, after that he wouldn't even shoot a coyote. Never talked about it, but I could tell killing that wolf had changed him, and I guess it did me too."

Clay didn't know what to say, and wasn't sure why Mr. Darling was telling him these things.

"Clay, we're sure pleased you'll be here to take in the county fair with us. It starts with the dance tomorrow evening out at Dance Hall Rock—it's to commemorate the dances that the pioneers held there back in 1879. They were on their way to Hole-in-the-Rock, to cross the Colorado and start a mission up the San Juan. Anyway, I wanted to ask if you'd help me with the chuck wagon tomorrow afternoon. We'll go out there in the old style and get the barbecue started with some other fellows, and Mrs. Darling and the girls will drive out a little later with the side dishes and all. Would you do that with me?"

Clay didn't understand why Sarah's father was being so formal. "Sure," Clay said. "Happy to."

Mr. Darling didn't say anything for a while, then at last he said, "After that meeting we were at this evening, I had a chance to visit with my brother, the sheriff. I don't know how else to tell you this, but you deserve to know, so I'm just going to have to come out and say it. There's some news about your uncle that isn't so good."

How bad? Clay thought. How bad?

"Barlow has some connections in Salt Lake. He's succeeded in having another court hear your uncle's case rather than ours here, on the grounds that this is a small town and everyone's too worked up on one side or the other. What that means is, your uncle's going to be moved way up to Salt Lake."

"How soon?" Clay asked desperately.

"Day after tomorrow . . . I know you're disappointed, but I'm glad you got to visit him—"

"Can I see him in the morning?"

"I'd sure think so. My brother's disappointed that it's worked out like this. . . . Maybe your mom, as soon as she gets back, can find the best lawyer possible for him."

"How bad is it? How much trouble is he in?"

Mr. Darling looked away, and thought awhile, and then he looked back. "No telling yet, but it doesn't look good. There's a chance he'll have to serve time in the state prison. Make an example out of him, that kind of thing. To tell you the truth, I wish he'd managed to get away last week when they first caught him. If he could have made it back onto the reservation and across the Arizona border . . . This sort of offense they wouldn't bother to extradite a man for. Likely wouldn't be any more trouble if he just stayed out of the state."

21

"Sarah's in the root cellar, Clay," Mrs. Darling said, and pointed across the yard. Her eyes were asking how the early morning visit at the jail had gone, but she knew that's why he wanted to see Sarah. "Clay, would you take that box of jars in the kitchen down to Sarah? Those tomatoes are heavy."

In the shade of an immense cottonwood tree, steps led down to a door at the front of a long mound of earth. Sarah looked up when he came in. Her beautiful smile was mixed with worry.

"Tomato delivery," Clay said as bravely as he could. Really, he wanted to cry. But he'd cried on his own outside the jail, and what was happening was sad enough, he'd better not think about it too much or he'd start crying again.

She was labeling a canning jar filled with some kind of long unsightly vegetables. "What is that stuff?" he asked, and wrinkled his nose.

"Pickled okra. We're going to enter it in the fair."

He picked up a jar of cherries she'd also labeled and set with other jars she'd singled out. "If they need tasters, I'll volunteer for these, but I'll pass on that okra stuff. My mom says I have a rule—if it sounds funny and looks weird, it can't be good to eat."

Remember, Clay told himself. You told your uncle how much you were looking forward to the dance, and you even told him about Sarah's new dress. "This dance tonight is going to be extra special for Sarah," Uncle Clay had said. Don't spoil it for her was what he meant.

He was looking around at the shelves upon shelves of canned fruits and vegetables. It was staggering how much food her family had stored away. "It sure is cool in here," he said absently.

"I like your new boots, Clay. Did your uncle see them?"

"No, I got 'em on the way home."

She was placing the tomatoes on the shelves. "My father told me what's happened," she said. "How is your uncle Clay?"

He had to share his heart with her. His lip was quivering but there wasn't anything he could do about it. If he couldn't tell her how he felt, who would he ever be able to talk to? "My uncle was trying to be brave about it, but I could tell how bad he felt. I just don't think you can lock up somebody like him. You know what he said? 'Freedom's the air I breathe.' "

"I know, I've been thinking what that would be like. There wouldn't be anything more awful."

"I feel so . . . useless."

"You made him happy—you came all this way to find him. I'm sure you lifted his spirits this morning."

Clay's eyes returned to the pen in her hand. "I didn't mean to keep you from labeling those."

"I'm just about done," she said, and wrote "August 1962."

"I can't believe how much food you have down here."

"It's part of being in our church," she explained. "Every family has a year's supply of food stored away. There's flour in those barrels over there, cornmeal, and rice, and in the sawdust bins, apples and potatoes."

"I guess you'll be in good shape if there's an atomic war."

"That's part of it," she agreed. "Here, let me show you what's back here."

At the rear of the root cellar Sarah opened another door. It opened onto another room with four simple beds and a tiny kitchen with a counter, sink, and an old-fashioned cookstove.

"What's all this?"

"Our bomb shelter. Behind the partition there, there's even a little bathroom."

He felt awful. "That's nice," he said uncertainly. "You won't be able to go outside for a half a year or a year or something."

"I know. Even if we're not a target or anything, they say the radiation just falls out of the sky and poisons everything. But I don't think it's really going to happen, Clay."

He looked at the shelter. It said otherwise. He was never going to have the chance to do something great, like one of the people in President Kennedy's book, *Profiles in Courage*. "Seattle's going to get blown to kingdom come," he said.

Sarah said with conviction, "I don't think so."

"Why not, then?"

"It's like last winter when John Glenn's capsule was returning into the atmosphere, and for a few minutes there was no radio contact and they were wondering if the heat shield came off the capsule and he'd burned up. Did you think he was going to be okay or that he'd been killed?"

"I thought he was going to make it. I was praying like anything."

"So was I, and I thought he was going to make it too. If we were always going around afraid . . . We wouldn't even be able to go to Dance Hall Rock this evening. We'd have to stay close to our bomb shelter in case anything happened!"

There she'd done it, she'd made him smile again. That long braid swung as she closed the door and turned toward her canning jars. He wanted to reach out and touch that braid, but he watched it go. "Let's get back to work," Sarah said. "Let's box up these things we're going to enter in the fair so they're ready tomorrow morning. If you think I've got ribbons you ought to see Mom's. If we're lucky, maybe she's made an extra pie while she was baking the ones for the fair."

"Sarah, what will happen to the horses now, the ones we hid in Death Hollow?"

"I don't know, Clay, I just don't know. Maybe I'll have to go back and let them go."

Outside, Libby and Nora were riding Pal, and Burrito was trotting alongside. "Look Sarah," Libby shouted. "Dad's going to let us ride in to the fair tomorrow on Pal if it's okay with Clay!"

"You bet it is," he called.

Clay looked at Sarah. She sure was fond of her sisters. It seemed like the three of them should have a brother.

Wait a minute, he told himself. What am I thinking about! Not in a million years would I begin to feel for Sarah like a *brother*!

It was a goodly distance out to Dance Hall Rock. Clay was riding Starbuck alongside the chuck wagon, an old covered wagon full of the pots and pans and other paraphernalia needed to put on the big feed before the dance. Now and again Mr. Darling would cluck to the team of four horses and give the reins a snap. Like his daughter, that man knew how to cluck to a horse without coming off like a chicken.

A friend of Mr. Darling's was seated on the wagon bench with him so Mr. Darling wasn't lacking for company. In between them stood Curly with his little front feet up on Mr. Darling's legs, commanding a view of the team and the road and panting as if he didn't have that canvas shade over his head. Clay was happy to have the time to himself to think, to just let himself go with the rhythm of the saddle and drift off the way he liked.

He drifted off a couple different directions, but he would never drift very far until he returned to the man in the cell. Tomorrow Uncle Clay would be sent up to Salt Lake City and he'd be put in a jail that wasn't like the Escalante jail at all. There'd be no Aunt Violet there who knew he wasn't the kind who should be in jail and treat him kindly. How long would he be in prison? Pretty long, Mr. Darling had implied. You could see it written all over her father's face. How long? Three years, five years, ten years? Even three would be forever.

In three years I'll be out of high school, Clay thought. That's so far away you can't even begin to picture it.

What about the salmon fishing they were going to do? What about the boat up to Ketchikan, Alaska? When he'd found his uncle it felt like they were just getting started. His uncle had seen he wasn't a little kid anymore.

Or was he a little kid? Growing tall, but still a kid.

There was something that was nagging at the edge of his memory like a raven squawking when you're coming out of a nap in the shade. What was it? Something important. Oh, well.

Dance Hall Rock sits in some pretty country, he thought. Yucca and junipers, red sand, dunes and rolling slickrock, rock outcrops of red and pink and white sandstone. A lot like Monument Valley, really. He wondered if they'd ever made any Westerns here. Well, they should.

It was something Mr. Darling had said, he realized. That's what was nagging at him and demanding to be remembered. When her father had been talking about Uncle

Clay, when he'd been talking about him getting caught—
that was it. "He'd be all right as long as he didn't come
back to the state of Utah." That was it, that's what he'd
said.

Uncle Clay needs to get out of there, Clay thought.
That's what he really needs. He needs a good old-fashioned
escape. All he needs is to ride through these dunes and over
this slickrock and out of this town and this state.

That's what he should really be doing, figuring out how
to bust his uncle out of jail.

But how would you pull it off? Could that even be
possible?

He must have seen a thousand jailbreaks. . . . If he
could only remember, one of them would show him the
way. What would John Wayne do? How about hitching up
Starbuck to the bars in Uncle Clay's cell window, the little
one at ground level in the window well? What if he hitched
up Pal too? What if he used this team of four that Mr.
Darling was driving?

Who was he fooling? He'd seen those bars. The ones
they use for the movies must be hollow or something.

What about dozing deputies? More than any other ploy,
that was the one that seemed to work the most often. Figure
out how to sneak the keys right off a dozing deputy or from
right under their nose. With a broom handle and a little
nail bent at a right angle sticking out of the end of it, he
could lift that big key ring right off the end of the dozing
deputy's sleepy fingers. . . .

Wait a minute! The deputy in this case was Aunt Violet,
and she was never dozing. She was always sweeping or
mopping or cooking or something. Not only that, she didn't
have one of those big old movie key rings with all the giant
keys. She only had an ordinary little key ring with four or
five keys on it, probably her car key and house key and her
jail keys. And she didn't keep them where you could send

164

Curly after them or snag them with your fishing line and a hook—she always kept them in her dress pocket.

"There it is," Mr. Darling called.

"What?" he replied, half-startled.

"Dance Hall Rock. Say, did you fall asleep on your horse?"

"Just kind of daydreaming," he replied.

To himself, he added: "As usual."

Clay helped unload the chuck wagon, and then he had a chance to inspect the "dance floor." It was easy enough to picture those pioneers at this natural slickrock pavilion, and it was easy to imagine how perfectly the huge sandstone backdrop projected the sounds of the instruments back to the dancers.

In a minute Clay had an ax in his hands and he was helping to make kindling and to lay it into the barbecue pits. Right on cue a pickup pulled in full of seasoned scrub oak and he helped to get the fires going. In another half hour the folding tables and chairs arrived and he went to work setting them up on the slickrock. The men and the boys were dressed in their newest jeans and best shirts, dress boots and go-to-church Stetsons. They were kind of shy about talking to him, but they were happy to have him working alongside. It was good to have something to do, to keep his mind off tomorrow.

Some of the younger boys couldn't keep their eyes off his jewelry. That's what set him apart from them, and the fact he was a stranger of course. Everybody around Escalante knew everybody else. He heard several whisper, "That's Clay Jenkins's nephew."

The meat was brought out soaking in barbecue sauce, in dozens and dozens of deep metal pans.

It was late afternoon now and the whole town was driving in, the whole county. He had a giant pair of gloves on and a huge fork in his hands, and he was helping tend the beef over the red-hot coals. It felt awful good working alongside Mr. Darling. It felt good to see all the women arriving with their colorful dresses and their hair all done up, and going right to work spreading out tablecloths on the tables and laying out more food on the buffet lines that he'd ever seen in one place. There were kids running around, excited as baby burros, hundreds of kids.

He asked Mr. Darling, "How many cows are we cooking up here?"

Before Clay heard an answer, his eye caught Libby and Nora and Mrs. Darling and a fourth with them, a young woman with wavy dark hair all down her back and a flower in her hair. All were wearing long dresses and carrying dishes of food toward the buffet tables. Who was that young woman, or was it a girl, in the rose-colored dress. . . .

Then he realized—Sarah! You fool, it's Sarah, with her hair all combed out down her back. That's Sarah, in the dress she made!

22

They sat down right across the picnic table from one another. At first Clay was so taken with how different Sarah looked, he could barely look at her. All he could do was eat; he was good at that, and he'd heaped his plate high. He was beginning to feel he didn't know her at all, didn't belong here, when Sarah said, "I wish you could see the colors next month up around Cyclone Lake, when the aspens are turning."

What a relief to hear her speak. She was still the same Sarah. She was real, not someone he'd dreamed up. Now he couldn't take his eyes off her, this girl in the rose-colored dress with the embroidered flowers at her neck, this girl with the long wavy dark hair all glistening. He was going to miss her so badly, it hurt already. How much longer could he stay? Another week?

"There's Uncle Dave," Libby said, pointing out the man in the starched uniform returning from seconds at the grill.

The sheriff, Clay realized. He looks so stiff, and so official. It was hard to imagine he'd been sympathetic with Uncle Clay.

"Their family always sits with us," Libby said. "How come they didn't this year?"

"The election's coming up soon, and he has to campaign," Mrs. Darling said. "He has to mix with everybody."

"And there's that Mr. Barlow," Nora sang out. "He's worse than Liberty Valance."

"Shush, now," Mrs. Darling said. "Nora, see if your father's got enough help so he can come sit down with us yet."

"Clay, let's get some dessert," Sarah suggested.

The sun had set. The slickrock in the distance, out toward the Colorado, was rimmed with orange. Guitars and fiddles were tuning up, a banjo too.

They ran into Aunt Violet dishing out slices from the homemade pies. She was wearing one of those ruffled dresses and she had her gray hair piled up extra high with a purple ribbon to match the dress. She broke into a big smile when she saw him. This felt like running into somebody you knew from home. "You look great tonight, Aunt Violet," Clay told her.

"I'm going to take some of these back to your uncle," she said. "One of each kind, so he can take his choice and eat as much as he wants. I hope you came to dance, Clay— you're going to see quite a shindig here tonight."

He could tell she was trying to cheer him up. She knew too, what was going to happen in the morning.

The band looked like they were ready, but then they set their instruments aside. "There's going to be a few speeches," Sarah explained.

They drifted away from the speeches toward a nearby rock formation, where they sat and watched quietly. The moon was just about to rise across the Colorado. He reached for her hand as they watched the moon lift huge and orange from those slickrock badlands between the two rivers. The full moon freed itself from the rock ocean and buoyed up enormous and bright and orange into the night sky. She squeezed his hand. They looked at each other, knowing each other's hearts. Curly appeared from the busy rounds he'd been making and jumped up on their laps, offering his moist black nose.

The speeches were short, and the band soon launched into a full-speed-ahead "Orange Blossom Special." Sarah's feet began to tap. It was easy to see she was looking forward to dancing, and Clay guessed it wasn't going to be any sort of dancing he could manage. They walked over closer to the dance floor and watched.

The next number slowed things down some, and the people didn't wait to be invited to commemorate the dances that the pioneers had held on this very spot so many years before. Clay and Sarah stood to the side and watched the men twirl their partners gracefully. The petticoats were flying. A harmonica player joined in and Clay thought of his friend Russell and the Midnight Flyer and the campfire that night when he'd tried to dance their way and only ended up creating his own unique style. This kind of dancing was just as foreign to him as Navajo dancing.

Her parents joined in at the next dance. Aunt Violet was out there too, and she was quite a dancer. To Clay's horror, a boy came up and asked Sarah for the next dance. To his everlasting relief she shook her head, and the boy disappeared. "That was George Winchell," she said, "from school."

"Sarah," he said. "I'm not sure I can do this kind of dancing, but I'll give it a try."

"Let's practice a little right here, first. I'll teach you."

"Really, right here?"

He concentrated hard. With your hands on her hips, or with your fingers entwined, you signaled what you were going to do, and then you just did it. She was making it seem easy. Before long he was twirling her too, and those layers of pink and white ruffles were swirling like a top. Then they joined the other dancers. Her long hair was

169

flying, and she was looking into his eyes. It didn't matter if he lost the beat; he could find it again. It was so crowded, nobody was really watching anybody else and there were collisions besides the ones he caused. It all seemed to be part of the fun. "You're so lucky to live here, Sarah . . . ," he said all out of breath. "Everyone in town must be out here tonight."

"Escalante's deserted," she agreed.

Except for my uncle, he thought. In the basement of the Escalante courthouse. One man down there very much alone.

Aunt Violet swept by with an elderly gentleman a head shorter than she. She was having the time of her life.

Aunt Violet's not at the jail, he thought. Aunt Violet's here. She's your dozing deputy. . . . She's the key. . . . *She's got the keys!*

Clay tried to steer Sarah toward Aunt Violet. He was working on an idea and it was firing him all up inside like a Roman candle. He got a pretty good glimpse of Aunt Violet again, but he couldn't tell for sure what he needed to know. "Sarah," he whispered, "I need to talk to you."

He tugged her away from the dancers, and then he whispered in her ear, "Would Aunt Violet's dress have a pocket, like the ones she wears at work?"

"Mine does." Sarah's hand slipped between folds in the pattern of her dress on the right side, and he could see the white of the lining there. "How come you're wondering?"

Clay's eye was still on Aunt Violet, wheeling there among the dancers. She always kept the keys in her dress pocket. Of course she'd have them with her. That's where she kept them. This dress would have a pocket too. It had to.

The song was ending. It was crazy, but if he was going to try it he better not think about it too long, he better do it now. "Watch," he said. "Stay right here. I'll be back in a few minutes."

170

Clay squeezed between couples getting their breath. You'll only have one chance, he told himself. I don't think she's left-handed. Her pocket would be on her right side. Try her right side.

Aunt Violet's partner was thanking her for the dance. Clay presented himself. "May I have the next dance?" he asked as gallantly as possible and all out of breath.

She was delighted. She probably thinks I can dance, Clay thought.

It was a pretty fast dance, a "Texas swing dance" as he heard Aunt Violet remark, and he swung himself into it and swung her too, like a whirling dervish. The Navajos would've loved this! Aunt Violet was smiling through it at least. She had a nervous smile you might expect from someone at the top of a carnival ride that's a lot scarier than they expected.

When Clay had things wound up as much as he could wind them, he gave Aunt Violet a huge spin and stuck out the tip of his cowboy boot below her flying dress to catch her ankle, and then he lunged to make sure she would land on him, which is what she was doing. He was enveloped by her skirts and reaching for that pocket even before she went down. To Aunt Violet it might have seemed he was thrashing around trying to escape her considerable weight; to him all the motion was meant to camouflage the job of the one limb he was counting on, his right arm and his right hand.

He had the keys! And yes, his hand was free of her pocket and those keys were tucked in his own jeans before all the confusion came to rest. People close by were standing around, some chuckling. The band was playing on, thank goodness, and he was apologizing all over himself to Aunt Violet who was dusting herself off. "I'm pretty dangerous," he said, snugging his hat back on his head.

"That you are," she agreed.

"This kind of dancing's all new to me. But you should see me do the Twist."

"Another time, Clay," she said, laughing now. "Another time."

That lady wasn't going to let one fall spoil her evening. Her partner was back to save her, and she went right on dancing.

Clay whispered in Sarah's ear, "I want to show you something." A little ways into the moonlight, he took her hand and led her toward the formation where they'd watched the moon rise. A little ball of white joined them. "Curly!" Clay said. "Stick close, now."

Behind the rock formation he pulled the keys out of his pocket. "Sarah," he said. "These are Aunt Violet's keys. The keys to the jail and Uncle Clay's cell."

She gasped.

"Uncle Clay's horse is in the corral right by the jail. We can make it to Arizona. I have to try."

"The sheriff will come after you, and Barlow will too."

"They won't find out until sometime after the dance. I figure it'll be hard to track us if we stay on the slickrock."

"You're right about that. I'm sure they'll come in their trucks, on the road. . . . With the moonlight, you could ride at night and hide in the canyons by day. . . . I think you'd have a chance anyway, Clay."

"Sarah, I have to go fast, I have to get back to town as fast as I can."

He reached out for her. The moon lit up the yellow flecks in her eyes. Clay touched her cheek with one hand, and his other hand found the silkiness of her hair. His lips touched hers, and then their lips met, and it felt like . . . canyons and mesas and rainbows, and the desert fresh after a rain. It felt like the promise of the life that lay before him all shining and ready for him to make something of. "I love you," he whispered. "Sarah Darling, Sarah Darling."

172

"I love you, Clay. I really love you."

They held hands. "I just got here," he said, and a tear popped out of an eye. "I just met you."

"I know. . . ."

"Say good-bye to your folks for me, and Libby and Nora. They won't mind keeping Pal and Burrito for me, will they?"

"Pal and Burrito will be eating at the table."

"It'll be good to know exactly where those desert canaries are. And I'm going to come back and see them."

"You better," she sniffled. "And take care of yourself, Clay. Remember, there's no one else like you."

"Do you like letters? Long ones?"

"The longer the better."

He took the silver bracelet with the three beautiful stones from his wrist and he put it on hers. "It's a little big," he said.

Sarah slid it up her arm some. "Fits perfect."

He kissed her again, and then their lips parted, and then Clay stood up to leave.

"But I want to see you once more," Sarah was saying. "Maybe there's a chance. I know where you'll be going, I can try to guess how long it might take you. . . . Be sure to look around for me before you cross the Colorado. I just might be there."

Clay tucked Curly to his chest so no one would notice the ball of white. As he walked his horse away from the music echoing out of Dance Hall Rock, he could hear the band singing, "A-way, I'm bound a'way, a-cross the wide Mis-sour-i."

Missouri nothing, Clay thought as he mounted Starbuck and nestled Curly in his left hand against his stomach. Across the Colorado and into the reservation. *Across the Colorado and into Arizona!*

173

23

By night, they rode. Late in the night that first night, they saw the headlights of vehicles prowling around on the slickrock. But it was a big country and none came close enough to cast its lights on them. Occasionally they'd encounter a cluster of cows taking in the moonlight, and Curly would bark under his breath. Clay explained to Uncle Clay that they must be those "10–30" cows.

Whenever their horses left a pile of evidence behind, Uncle Clay brought his gloves out of his saddlebags and buried it in a patch of sand. He was being that careful. "I won't give Barlow much credit, but I'm guessing he knows the difference between cow pies and horse apples. You know, Clay, we're just like two Apaches. On all this slickrock, they'll never find us."

"I sure hope not," Clay said with a feeling of dread. His uncle was feeling awful good, but was he being realistic?

"Lemme tell you about Apaches," Uncle Clay said, with a wild glint of moonlight in his eye. "They say, out in the middle of the desert with just rocks and sand, and scrub around no taller than your waist, you could turn your back on an Apache and he could disguise himself no farther'n a

174

stone's throw away, disguise himself so well you just plain couldn't find him."

"Is that true?"

"I wouldn't doubt it. There's so much we don't know. . . . Those colors in your saddle blanket, they all come from the plants around here. Those Navajo women know exactly which ones, and whether its the roots or leaves or flowers. . . . We're bound for Yazzieland, Clay! I still can't believe you busted me out of the Escalante jail!"

"You should've seen the look on your face."

"Man oh man . . . God I love this country!"

By day they hid in one of the many slot-canyons that drained toward the Escalante, and they ate from the grub they'd pilfered from the jail kitchen and stashed in their saddlebags. They napped in the shade, but Clay never really slept. He kept listening for the sound of approaching horses, or footsteps. He knew they were out there, the sheriff and Barlow too.

When the moonlight showed on the canyon wall above, they started out of the canyon. Uncle Clay held the horses while Clay sneaked up to the rim and looked all around, keeping low to the ground. Curly knew to keep quiet. All clear. Before long they were up on the slickrock again, riding on the rolling sea of slickrock.

After several hours they heard vehicles, jeeps or trucks, and saw their profiles far off. They were running without headlights this time. "Stay still," Uncle Clay said.

"They'll see us!" Clay whispered. "If we can see them, they can see us."

"Not necessarily," Uncle Clay said. "If we stay real still, from that distance we're going to look like a couple of these junipers."

The motors droned away in the distance, just as Uncle Clay had predicted.

A second day they hid, and another night they rode.

With daylight approaching once again, Clay steered for the safety of a nearby canyon. "This way," his uncle said, staying on the beeline across the exposed slickrock toward the east and the lavenders of dawn.

"But Uncle Clay . . . ," he warned, "they can see us up here."

"We're going to be all right," his uncle said, only a little bit tense. "They're going to be tired of looking for us by now. They've gone home for breakfast."

"I sure hope so."

Why were they taking such a chance? Clay thought. It wasn't worth it! They were so close, so close now.

They rode for another half hour. Clay's dread was growing as the daylight was coming on. "It's getting really light, Uncle Clay!"

"Just a little bit farther," his uncle replied. His uncle looked worried now too, but his jaw was set.

Clay was looking all around, all around, and listening. Was he hearing a motor or was he just imagining it?

Still they continued on. The sun was rising. Off to the southeast, he could see a big corral. "Please, Uncle Clay, let's get out of here."

"Just up ahead," was all his uncle said.

As soon as Clay saw this canyon, he didn't have a good feeling about it. It didn't look deep enough or narrow enough to do them much good. It was more like a broad wash. You could see into the bottom of it from a long ways.

"It gets deep soon enough," his uncle said reassuringly.

They started down into the wash. Still, Clay didn't like it. There was no way down on slickrock like there had been into the canyon the day before. They were leaving all kinds of tracks. Why take a risk like this?

They followed the wash downstream until the walls rose

a hundred feet. Still, the wash was wide, and someone up above would see everything. "Let's hurry," he said.

"We'll be okay." His uncle reined his horse in. "Right here. This is a stop I have to make, Clay."

Without saying another word, his uncle tied his horse to a bush right there in the bottom of the wash and started climbing up the hillside.

Clay didn't know what he should do. They had to get down this canyon and fast, and get onto some slickrock where they couldn't be followed. Curly was looking back and forth between him and his uncle moving up the slope, and he was confused too.

Clay scrambled up the slope after him. His uncle was crouching up there at the base of the rimrock where a big slab of rock had fallen down and was leaning back against the rimrock.

He was breathing hard when he reached his uncle. He paused for a second to catch his breath. The soil was dusty and loose, like you find around the cliff ruins. His uncle was crouching at the entrance of the tentlike space under the leaning slab, and he'd taken his hat off. There was a pile of rocks in there, and something else. . . .

Clay leaned closer, and then he saw it. The All-Around Cowboy buckle tucked back in the rocks.

"I had to stop, Clay. I sure hope it isn't going to get us caught, but if I'm never going to come back into this state I knew I had to pay her a visit, one last time."

"I'll run up and keep a lookout," Clay said hurriedly. As much as anything, he thought he should give his uncle privacy for his grief.

It was a a few hundred yards back up the canyon before he found a way up and out. It was broad daylight now and he was terrified. As he was nearing the rim he kept to his belly and crawled up like a lizard. All he meant to do was poke his head over the top.

Up ahead, Curly was growling.

"Quiet, Curly!"

A little ways farther, and he'd be able to peek over the top.

What he found was a big man standing just back from the rim. A man with a deer rifle, a man with a face hard like an anvil and unshaven. A jeep was parked three or four hundred yards away, back by the corral.

"Thought you were pretty smart, didn't you?" The man's voice was hoarse and pitiless.

Clay didn't say anything. All his hopes were dust. Clay stood up and came over the rim, looked around. There was no one but Barlow.

"The sheriff wouldn't stick with it," Barlow sneered. "I knew you were out here somewhere. Your uncle's a rodeo cowboy, that's all he is. I was born out here."

Down the canyon, Uncle Clay had his back turned and wasn't seeing this. He was in the same crouched position. Should he shout to his uncle? Would Barlow shoot? Would Uncle Clay run even if he could?

Uncle Clay wouldn't run with me up here, Clay realized. There's nothing I can do. It's all over.

"Look, Mr. Barlow, why don't you just let him go? He never hurt you, I mean, not you personally."

The man snorted in disgust, and then squinted down the canyon. "What's he doing over there? He's been in that same spot for fifteen minutes."

"Visiting her grave," Clay said quietly.

"Whose grave?" Barlow's voice was harsher than ever.

"Don't you remember? When he came to you to get horses, and his wife was sick? You said she'd just eaten too much frybread, or something like that? Don't you remember?"

Clay saw confusion in Barlow's face at first, and then the memory coming back.

178

"They think her appendix burst. She died out here."

"I never knew that," Barlow said roughly. "I never heard that from anybody."

"He never talks about it," Clay said. "I learned it from the Navajos."

Barlow stared a long time down the canyon at the man under the rimrock. Then his hard features slackened as the hatred seemed to leave his eyes for a moment. "I'll tell you what, kid . . . ," Barlow said finally, still looking down the canyon. "Just get him out of here . . . just get him out of here for good."

The man turned suddenly on his heel and walked away.

For a moment Clay almost said thanks. No, it was better to say nothing. Even to Uncle Clay, he'd say nothing of what had happened here.

Hurry him down to the river, today. The sheriff might still come looking.

"Now that we've left tracks in this canyon, let's just skedaddle," Uncle Clay said. His eyes were bright and shining but the dust on his cheeks showed the passage of tears. "This is the start of Coyote Canyon. If we keep moving all day, I believe we can cross the river yet this afternoon."

"Fine with me," Clay said. "Let's make tracks, Uncle Clay. Let's make tracks, Curly. I told Russell Yazzie I was going to come back and see him one day—wait till he finds out how soon!"

"A couple days of hard riding and we'll be there. I can smell that wooly mutton roasting from here."

"And I'm going to have a decent present to give my friend."

"What's that?"

"His horse back!"

They dropped into a deeper and deeper canyon. They rode under a natural bridge and they rode under Lobo Arch.

They rode under hanging gardens of ferns and red wildflowers, and dripping springs so convenient they stuck out their mouths and drank from horseback. When they reached the canyon of the Escalante they turned downstream along its sandy shallows.

Past the mouth of Davis Canyon they rode, and Clay remembered a cloudburst and a burro being born. All the while he was scanning the rims a thousand feet above, looking for a girl waving where he guessed she'd be. Soon they'd leave her country and his heart would be left behind as well.

Between the sheer red walls they rode, between the waving willows at the Escalante's edge. No cloudburst coming today. The sky was as blue as the walls were red and the willows were green. "*Bik'é Hozhoni*," he said aloud.

"Yes, sir," his uncle agreed. "On the beautiful trail we go."

"Just a couple of miles to the river," Clay said, looking up to the rims. "We aren't safe yet."

At last, the coffee-and-cream Colorado. They reined their horses in, and his uncle reached over and shook his hand. "I'll never forget it, Clay. And what do you keep looking up for, anyway?"

"Oh, I'm just checking out the canyon. It sure is deep." In fact, it was so deep he couldn't see up to the Escalante's rims. Even if she was up there he wouldn't see her.

Uncle Clay said it was important to rest the horses before the big swim across the river. They rested too, lying on the riverbank without speaking, thinking about all that had happened. Curly nestled his head against Clay's shoulder and sighed, then closed his eyes.

Just as Clay was thinking the horses must be rested enough and they shouldn't wait any longer, Curly lifted his head and looked around ominously. The tiny dog's brown ears were standing straight up. Clay listened too and thought he heard something, listened again.

At first it sounded far off, like the ocean in a conch shell. Strangely, it was building fast. Clay reached for his hat and got to his feet. Uncle Clay was hearing it too, and he was alarmed.

The sound was swelling, like the Pacific during a storm. In the time it took for Clay to scoop Curly up and turn toward the mustang, the roar was rushing his way, sounding more like a colossal torrent of hailstones, and it seemed to be coming at them off the Escalante's walls.

Clay was fumbling with his shirt buttons, trying to get Curly safely tucked inside for the swim across the river. Uncle Clay, standing by with both horses, was ready to hand him Starbuck's reins.

But before they could mount up, the torrent was upon them. Horses were streaming out of the Escalante and into the canyon mouth, riderless horses with their manes flying. In the lead, that mare blue as a mountain bluebird.

"Holy cow," his uncle said.

Then came the black-and-white dogs, and behind them, the girl on that palomino horse with her long braid flying.

"Got some horses for you!" she called.

Author's Note

While *The Big Wander* is a work of fiction, the idea of a boy, burro, and dog adventuring in the canyon country was inspired by the wanderings of Everett Ruess, a real-life artist and vagabond who has become a legendary figure in the Southwest. The tiny dog who rides the burro's pack in this story is named after Everett's dog, Curly, as a tribute to this remarkable young man who disappeared in the canyons of the Escalante in 1934. His fate remains a mystery.